TOMBSTONE

MATT BRAUN

St. Martin's Paperbacks

TOMBSTONE

Copyright © 1981 by Matthew Braun.

ISBN: 0-312-98177-5

Printed in the United States of America

Pocket Books edition / April 1981
Pinnacle edition / June 1985
St. Martin's Paperbacks edition / September 2002

St. Martin's Paperbacks are published by St. Martin's Press, 175 Fifth Avenue, New York, NY 10010.

10 9 8 7 6 5 4 3 2 1

TO THE ADAIRS

Dorothy and Harry

Eleanor and Bob

Peggy and Ham

AUTHOR'S NOTE

The gunfight at the OK Corral has become one of the more enduring myths in western folklore.

Yet, very few people realize that the OK Corral shootout was but a prelude. What occurred afterward represents one of the bloodiest chapters in the annals of the Old West.

Between October, 1881, and April, 1882, Tombstone became a battleground. A savage vendetta, triggered by the OK Corral gunfight, resulted in murder and assassination, and cold-blooded execution. There was never any question as to who did the killing, or why. There was controversy then as to Wyatt Earp's motives, and to some extent, that controversy still exists. Stripped of fabrication and myth, however, several startling truths have survived the passage of time.

The record rather conclusively demonstrates that greed and corruption, abetted by political ambition, were the root causes of the bloodletting. Stage robbery was epidemic, and Wyatt Earp was thought to be heavily involved, the mastermind behind an outlaw gang. Wells, Fargo actually sent two undercover agents into

Tombstone during this period. Their mission was to rout the gang and write an end to the bloodshed.

Luke Starbuck was uniquely qualified for such an assignment. His fame as a detective and manhunter was unrivaled in the Old West. The events depicted herein, and what he unearthed about Wyatt Earp, are for the most part documented fact. Some literary license has been taken regarding his method of operation and the actions of certain characters. All else is closer to the truth than the myth.

TOMBSTONE, through Luke Starbuck, tells the untold story.

CHAPTER 1

Starbuck angled across Larimer Street, one eye on the police station.

The Colt .45 stuffed in the waistband of his trousers gave him an uncomfortable moment. He was accustomed to enforcing the law, and the city ordinance against carrying firearms struck him as damnfool nonsense. His suit jacket concealed the gun, but he was still irked that progress had put him on the wrong side of the law.

Denver, like most western cities, considered itself a progressive metropolis. With 1881 drawing to a close, the population was approaching 100,000 and frontier customs were slowly losing ground to the civilized edicts of reformers. Not that old Denver had completely succumbed to the new cosmopolitan posture; graft and bribes still assured the discreet operation of whore-houses, gaming parlors, and busthead saloons. Yet it was now a hub of commerce, with two railroads and an expansive financial district. And a law against carrying guns.

Starbuck began wondering why he'd ever left

Texas. As he moved past the police station, it occurred to him that hindsight was the worst of all vantage points. However enlightening, it made a man feel very much the dimdot.

A brisk December wind whipped out of the northwest with biting force. He grunted, testing the wind for snow, and hurried along the street. Halfway down the block, he turned into the entrance of the Brown Palace Hotel.

In the lobby, he pulled out his pocket watch and checked the time. The letter from Vernon Whitehead had indicated ten sharp, and he still had a couple of minutes to spare. He inquired at the desk, and much as he'd expected, Whitehead's name commanded instant attention. The clerk pointed him in the right direction, all the while emphasizing that the gentleman in question occupied the hotel's finest suite. Starbuck crossed the lobby, gazing around at the ornate decor and a garish mural covering the breadth of the ceiling. He thought it beat the hell out of a bunkhouse.

Mounting the sweeping staircase, he was reminded that the whole operation had been organized on a large scale. Early next spring, the presidents of every cattlemen's association throughout the West would converge on Denver. Their purpose would be to unite in the formation of the International Cattlemen's Association. Their primary goal, aside from joining forces against homesteaders, would be an organized, far-reaching campaign directed at rustlers and horse thieves. Vernon Whitehead, chairman of the Executive Committee, had extended an invitation for him to attend a preliminary planning session. He was to be considered for the position of Chief Range Detective.

John Chisum, perhaps the most respected of all western cattlemen, had recommended him for the job. Some months earlier, he had been instrumental in disbanding a gang of rustlers who were preying on Chisum's vast New Mexico spread. At the same time, he'd had a hand in tracking down Billy the Kid, and was present the night Pat Garrett killed the young outlaw. The attendant publicity had advanced his already formidable reputation as a manhunter.

Upstairs, Starbuck proceeded along the hall and stopped before the door of the suite. He removed his hat, tugged the lapels of his jacket straight, and knocked. The murmur of voices inside quickly subsided, and a moment later the door opened. An older man, with a shock of white hair like candy floss, greeted him with an outstretched hand.

"You must be Luke Starbuck?"

"Yessir, I am. And you're—?"

"Vern Whitehead." Whitehead stepped aside. "C'mon in and meet the rest of the boys."

The suite was lavishly appointed. A thick Persian carpet covered the sitting room floor and grouped before the fireplace were several chairs and a plush divan. The other committee members—Sam Urschel, Oscar Belden, and Earl Poole—rose and moved forward. After a round of introductions, Whitehead motioned everyone to chairs.

There was no attempt at smalltalk. These men were ranchers, with little polish despite their wealth, and today they were all business. From the outset, it was apparent that Whitehead would act as spokesman for the group. Moreover, it was equally clear the interview would proceed along the lines of an interrogation.

Whitehead assessed him with a shrewd glance. "You as good as John Chisum says you are?"

Starbuck wasn't impressed. They obviously meant to put him on the defensive, and the tactic didn't sit well. He let them wait while he rolled a smoke. After flicking a match on his thumbnail, he took a long drag and exhaled.

"No offense intended, but you shouldn't have sent that invite unless you'd already checked me out."

"Oh, we checked you out, Mr. Starbuck. We can't afford to go on the say-so of nobody, not even John Chisum."

"Then I reckon you got all you need."

"Well, let's see." Whitehead extracted a sheaf of papers from inside his jacket. He snapped them open and began reading. "Says here you been a range detective since the summer of '76. Headquartered at Ben Langham's LX ranch, down in the Texas Panhandle. Worked out of there for the Panhandle Cattlemen's Association."

"Close enough." Starbuck admired the tip of his cigarette. "Except for the time I was out on loan to Chisum."

"Says here you've killed fourteen men."

"I never took time out to count."

Whitehead fixed him with an inquiring gaze. "Does fourteen include the ones you hung?"

"Nope." Starbuck looked at him without expression. "That would make it considerable higher."

"Not bad for a fellow"—Whitehead consulted his

notes—"who's just pushin' thirty-four. How is it a man your age ain't never been married?"

Starbuck smiled. "I like my work."

"Do you now?" Whitehead tapped the papers with his finger. "According to this, you inherited the LX from Langham and sold out to a bunch down in the Panhandle. That must've left you sittin' on easy street."

"I got enough to see me along."

"Hold on!" Oscar Belden interrupted. "You got money to burn, and you're tryin' to tell us you aim to keep on workin' for wages. Some of us find that a mite hard to swallow."

"I told you," Starbuck said in a deliberate voice. "I like my work. How much I've got in the bank doesn't concern you or anyone else. That's my business."

The words were spoken with the iron-sureness of a man who tolerated very little from others. Starbuck was a full six feet, but built along deceptive lines. He was lithe and corded, catlike in his movements, with a square jaw and lively chestnut hair. Five years as a range detective had brutalized him, and the vestiges of a violent trade were etched around his eyes. He had the steely gaze of someone who stayed alive by making quick estimates. And now, staring at the men, he wasn't at all certain he wanted the job. They seemed far too picky to suit his style.

"Let's suppose," Whitehead resumed, "that we offered you the job. Could you recruit ten or twelve good men and teach 'em to follow orders, no questions asked? I'm talkin' about a squad of detectives that would go wherever they're needed and do whatever they're told."

"All depends."

"On what?"

"On who gives the orders," Starbuck said flatly. "I take assignments, but I don't take orders. Either I do it my own way or I don't do it at all."

"John Chisum"—Whitehead paused as though weighing his words—"told us you was strong-headed. We might be willin' to give you the leeway needed, if you was willin' to hold yourself accountable to the Executive Committee."

"I take it you mean yourself and these other gents?"

"Most likely," Whitehead acknowledged. "Course, nothin's official till the Association gets itself formed next spring. But that's the way it stacks up right now."

"Exactly what was it you had in mind that needs ten or twelve men?"

"Killin'," Whitehead said bluntly. "We wouldn't object if you brought in a few for trial, but we'd sooner see a thief hung than sent to prison."

"Sounds like you mean to form a death squad."

"Altogether I reckon ranchers lose a couple of million dollars a year in rustled stock. We aim to put a stop to it, and I don't know no better way than the gallows tree."

Starbuck unfolded slowly from the divan. There was a slight bulge over the sixgun in his waistband, and he adjusted his suit jacket. Then he looked from man to man, nodding last to Whitehead.

"I'll let you know."

Before the cattlemen quite realized his intent, he

turned and walked to the door. The interview was concluded.

On the way downstairs Starbuck made a snap judgment. The job wasn't for him. There was no denying the honor involved; as Chief Range Detective his prestige among cattlemen would be greatly enhanced. Nor were there any qualms about the killing. The past five years had hardened him to the sight of death. Hanging a man wasn't pleasant, but neither was it repugnant. It was simply a function to be performed swiftly, an object lesson for those who robbed and murdered with godlike impunity. As for shooting a man who was trying to shoot him, there was no thought, no stirring of emotion, certainly no regret. He survived by allowing no man to threaten his life.

So the job itself wasn't what bothered him. He was concerned instead about Vernon Whitehead. Some gut instinct told him the rancher had lied. He sensed that Whitehead would say anything—promise anything— to gull him into accepting the job. Further, he felt there was something of the tyrant about Whitehead. Though it hadn't surfaced during the interview, the telltale signs were there. The rancher, little by little, would begin issuing orders rather than assignments. Eventually, like a drill sergeant, he would demand blind obedience and unquestioning loyalty. All of which meant they would come to loggerheads. Somewhere down the line Whitehead would show his true colors, and there would then be no choice but to sever the arrangement. It hardly seemed worth the effort, or the aggravation.

Then, too, there was no rush to accept the first job offered. As one of the committee members had pointed out, he wasn't exactly hurting for money. Upon the death of Ben Langham, an old friend and something of a surrogate father, he had inherited the largest cattle spread in the Panhandle. Yet, even though Langham had thought to cure his wanderlust, the responsibility was ill-suited to his character. Some inner restlessness made it impossible for him to become tied down to people, or things. He traveled light and he traveled alone, obligated to no one but himself. Satisfied with his life, and under no great compulsion to change, he had sold the ranch only last month. The proceeds—some $200,000—was stashed away in a bank in Fort Worth. The interest alone was enough to cover his immediate needs, with plenty to spare for an occasional whirl at the sporting life. And that afforded him the independence to do whatever he damn well pleased. Especially where it concerned work.

By the time he reached the lobby, Starbuck had decided he wanted no part of the International Cattlemen's Association. He wasn't sure where the decision would lead, nor was he overly concerned about the future. His reputation was established, and there was work anywhere in the West for a range detective who got results. Tomorrow was time enough to ponder his next move. For the moment, he had a definite yen to sample the nightlife of Denver. He'd heard there were parlor houses that specialized in Chinese girls. Young sloe-eyed Orientals, whose plumbing was reportedly vice-versa to that of white women. The mere thought galvanized him to a quicker pace.

Approaching the hotel entrance, Starbuck noticed a man leaning against the wall. Heavyset and thick through the shoulders, he wore a bowler hat perched atop his head like a bird's nest. He smiled, flashing a gold tooth, and stepped into Starbuck's path.

"Your name Starbuck?"

"Who's asking?"

"Mr. Griffin. Horace Griffin. He'd like to see you."

Starbuck started around him. "I don't know any Horace Griffin."

"He knows you."

"Where from?"

"Why not let him tell you himself? Mr. Griffin's Division Superintendent of Wells, Fargo—and that's all I'm authorized to say."

Starbuck stared at him a moment, then shrugged. "What the hell? Won't cost me nothing to listen."

The heavyset man smiled, indicating the door. Outside, they turned onto Larimer Street and set off at a brisk walk across town. Some ten minutes later they entered the Wells, Fargo & Company express station. There, Starbuck was ushered into a private office and greeted by a man who introduced himself as Horace Griffin. Solemn as a priest, Griffin wasted no time on amenities. He offered Starbuck a chair on the opposite side of the desk, and came straight to the point.

"Mr. Starbuck, I know all about your meeting with the Cattlemen's Association. If you've accepted the position, then I won't compromise you further. If not, then I have a proposition that may very well interest you."

"How'd you get wind of the meeting?"

"One of the members on the Executive Committee is a close personal friend. Which one really has no bearing on our discussion."

Starbuck eyed him, considering. "Suppose we just say I'm at loose ends."

"Fair enough," Griffin agreed. "I presume you've heard of Tombstone?"

"Arizona?"

Griffin nodded. "In the past year, we've had fourteen stages robbed in the Tombstone district. We carry express shipments and payroll boxes for the silver mines, so the losses have been substantial. Very substantial."

"Sounds like you've got yourself a problem."

"And getting worse." Griffin leaned forward, elbows on the desk. "Ten days ago our station agent in Tombstone disappeared."

"How do you mean—disappeared?"

"Vanished, Mr. Starbuck! Without a trace."

Starbuck looked interested. "Any chance he was involved in the robberies?"

"More than a chance," Griffin replied. "Have you ever heard of Wyatt Earp? Doc Holliday?"

"Seems like I read something in the papers a while back. Near as I recall, it involved a shootout of some sort."

"The press dubbed it the OK Corral Gunfight. Of course, that's neither here nor there. What does matter is that the Tombstone sheriff believes Earp and Holliday are behind the robberies. Unofficially, he also accused our agent, Marsh Williams, of being in league with them."

"And Williams suddenly disappeared."

"Precisely!"

"Has the sheriff brought charges?"

"Last year, shortly after one of the robberies, he arrested Holliday. All indications were that he had a good case. But the court dismissed the charges, even though there was strong circumstantial evidence. Coincidently, Holliday's three alleged accomplices have since been killed in unrelated holdups."

"So where do you stand now?"

"Facing a stone wall," Griffin said dourly. "We transferred another agent into Tombstone, but he reports it's hopeless. Everyone is convinced Wyatt Earp killed Williams, and they're afraid to talk. We have no case, no evidence, and no way to stop the robberies."

"I get the feeling you're offering me a job."

"We know of your work," Griffin ventured. "Please don't misunderstand me. I'm not referring to the men you've killed, but rather your investigative work. I was particularly impressed with the way you infiltrated that gang of horse thieves some years ago. Dutch Henry Horn, wasn't that the ringleader's name?"

"For a fact," Starbuck noted. "You've got a good memory."

"I'm also an excellent judge of character, Mr. Starbuck. Quite frankly, we need an undercover operative in Tombstone. I believe you're the man for the job."

Starbuck examined the notion. "I don't know beans from buckshot about stage robbers. What makes you think I could pull it off when your own people have failed?"

"Thieves are thieves," Griffin said equably. "Their mentality differs little, whether we're talking about horse thieves or stage robbers. You've demonstrated a knack for thinking the way they do, and uncovering the evidence to expose them. In all candor, I believe you were made to order for Tombstone."

There was a moment of calculation. Then Starbuck fixed him with a stern look. "I don't work cheap and I'm plumb set in my ways. I do it at my own speed and I don't follow nobody's rules. Not even Wells, Fargo."

"Have no fear," Griffin assured him earnestly. "I'll set no rules, and you can name your own compensation. Other than that, I have only two requests."

"Oh?" Starbuck's eyebrows rose in question. "What sort of requests?"

"First, keep me informed through Fred Dodge, the station agent in Tombstone. Second, end the robberies—by whatever means you deem expedient."

"Unless I heard wrong, you're authorizing me to catch them or kill them. Whichever works best."

"I am indeed, Mr. Starbuck! And the quicker the better."

"Mr. Griffin," Starbuck grinned and stuck out his hand. "You just hired yourself a detective."

Horace Griffin heaved himself to his feet. He grasped Starbuck's hand in a firm grip, and wished him luck in Tombstone. He thought it not only the best solution, but perhaps the only solution. Indeed for Wells, Fargo & Company, it made imminent good sense.

Hire a killer to catch a killer.

CHAPTER 2

A week later Starbuck crossed the line into Arizona Territory. From there, he followed a southerly route, skirting the Dragoon Mountains through Sulphur Spring Valley. Then he turned southwest, bypassing Tombstone, and angled generally in the direction of Nogales and the Old Mexico border. On a chill morning in late December, he rode into the headquarters of the San Bernardino Ranch.

John Slaughter, who laid claim to all the land within a day's ride, operated the ranch somewhat like a feudal empire. He was a law unto himself along the border, and his JHS brand was burned on some 40,000 cattle and 5,000 horses. A former Texas Ranger, he had settled in Arizona when it was still the domain of the Apache tribes. An implacable man, he had fought the Apaches and Mexican bandidos on their own terms, and ultimately created a kingdom where no renegade dared enter. Of greater consequence to Starbuck, he was an old and trusted ally of a mutual friend, John Chisum.

The main house was an immense adobe, squatting

somewhat like a fort around an open quadrangle. A veranda, shaded by an overhead gallery, spread across the width of the front wall. Starbuck dismounted, looping the reins of his roan gelding around a hitchrack, and slapped a cloud of dust off his mackinaw. As he walked toward the porch stairs, he noted that the window shutters, constructed of thick timber, were slitted with gun ports. He smiled, certain now that he'd judged the situation correctly. John Slaughter, not Tombstone, was the place to start.

A *mestizo* servant met him at the door, taking his hat and mackinaw. Then he was led down a corridor, his spurs jangling on the tile floor, and shown into a wolf's lair of a den. Saddles and range gear were strewn about the room, and the walls were lined by an impressive array of long guns. But the whole was dominated by a battered walnut desk, and the man who sat behind it.

Starbuck was surprised. From the tales he'd heard, he had expected Slaughter to be a giant of a man, sledge-shouldered and stout as an oak. Instead, the man circling the desk was below medium height, on the sundown side of thirty, with a slight paunch. Yet his whole bearing was charged with energy, and his face looked adzed from hard darkwood. His eyes were gray and intense, and Starbuck was suddenly reminded that a man's size often counted for nothing. Determination and grit, when all else was tallied, were the measure of a man's worth.

Slaughter halted, nodding amiably. "I'm John Slaughter."

"Luke Starbuck." Starbuck extended his hand.

"John Chisum told me to look you up whenever I got over your way."

"Why, hell, yes!" Slaughter pumped his arm with sudden enthusiasm. "You're the range detective. The one that helped ol' John nail Billy Bonney and clean out Lincoln County."

"Former range detective," Starbuck told him. "I'm with Wells, Fargo now."

"Well I'll be jiggered." Slaughter indicated chairs in front of a blazing fireplace. "Take a load off your feet and tell me all about it. You takin' over the relay operation, are you?"

Starbuck saw no reason to hedge. "Mr. Slaughter, I was hired as an undercover operative. They sent me down here to investigate Tombstone."

"Call me John." Slaughter lowered himself into a chair, suddenly somber. "Luke, I'm sorry to say they didn't do you no favors with that assignment. Not by a damnsight!"

"Amen," Starbuck said without irony. "Matter of fact, that's why I've come to see you, instead of heading directly into Tombstone. I thought maybe you could give me the lowdown on things."

"What things?"

"Wyatt Earp, just for openers. Wells, Fargo says him and Doc Holliday are behind all these stage hold-ups."

"Yeah, them and Bill Brocius."

"Brocius?"

"Curly Bill Brocius," Slaughter elaborated. "He's leader of the gang that actually pulls the holdups. Part of his bunch are the ones Earp murdered at the OK Corral."

"Murdered?" Starbuck was astounded. "I understood it was law business of some sort."

"Christ A'mighty, no! It was a falling out amongst thieves, plain and simple."

"How so?"

"Earp had the Wells, Fargo agent in his pocket. He got all the dope on payroll shipments and fed it to Brocius through Doc Holliday. The gang robbed the stages and afterward divvied up the take with Earp. Ain't nobody yet proved it, but you can bet your boots that's the way it worked."

"So what happened?"

"Well, now, that's a tale and then some. Takes a bit of tellin'."

"Fire away," Starbuck grinned. "I've got nowhere to go."

Slaughter hauled out a pipe and tobacco pouch. After fussing around, he got it filled and puffing to suit him. Then he leaned back, the pipe jutting from his mouth like a burnt tusk, and began to talk.

Wyatt Earp, along with his four brothers and Doc Holliday, had arrived in Tombstone the latter part of 1879. An ambitious man, and quick to talk about his days as a lawman in the Kansas cowtowns, Earp sought appointment as sheriff of Cochise County. Instead, the territorial governor appointed his chief rival, John Behan. Thoroughly disgruntled, Earp threw in with a group of gamblers and gunmen. At one time or another, their number included Luke Short, Bat Masterson, and Buckskin Frank Leslie. In the meantime, one of Wyatt's brothers, Virgil Earp, was twice defeated for the office of town marshal. Yet the second election produced the very ally the Earps needed. John Clum, editor of the weekly *Epitaph*, was elected mayor. Tombstone's other newspaper, the *Nugget*, was owned by Harry Woods, who supported Sheriff Behan. Earp and Clum, cast together as members of the opposing faction, soon became close friends. And the lines were drawn.

Shortly thereafter, the stagecoach robberies began. Though no hard proof existed, word leaked out that Earp had formed an alliance with Curly Bill Brocius. Among others, the Brocius gang included the Clanton brothers, the McLowery brothers, and the most dangerous *pistolero* in Arizona Territory, Johnny Ringo. Doc Holliday, on several occasions, was linked to the outlaw gang. But no solid evidence was uncovered, and therefore no connection to Earp could be established. The Earps gained a legal front, however, when the town marshal mysteriously departed Tombstone. Mayor Clum, now considered one of the family, appointed Virgil Earp to fill the post.

Then, over a period of months, mutual distrust between the Earps and the Brocius gang ripened into open hostility. Only two months ago, on October 26, it exploded in bloodshed. The Earp brothers and Doc Holliday cornered five of the gang at the OK Corral. Only two of the outlaws were armed, but that gave the Earps no pause. Within seconds, they killed three of the men; the others survived by dodging and running, all the while being fired on by Doc Holliday. In the aftermath, with the town council in a rebellious mood,

Virgil Earp was stripped of his marshal's badge. Wyatt and Doc Holliday were formally charged with murder, and eye-witness testimony substantiated that the killings had been performed in cold-blood. But Justice Wells Spicer, a political crony of the Earp-Clum faction, chose to ignore the facts. In his decision, notable for its convoluted logic, he absolved Earp and Holliday of all blame. The charges were dismissed.

After that, an eerie lull settled over Tombstone. The stage robberies abruptly ceased, and the Brocius gang hadn't appeared in town for more than a month. Earp and Holliday, conducting business as usual at the Alhambra Saloon, seemed to be biding their time. For what, no one had the faintest inkling. But everyone in Tombstone was convinced that Earp had yet another card up his sleeve. Despite his unsavory reputation, he was not noted as a quitter.

"That's the gist of it," Slaughter concluded, knocking the dottle from his pipe. "Earp and his crowd lost a little ground, but they ain't done yet. Not unless I miss my guess."

Starbuck digested what he'd heard, silent a moment. Then he looked up. "What about Fred Dodge, the new Wells, Fargo agent? Any chance Earp might try to work the same deal with him?"

"I'd tend to doubt it. After what happened to Marsh Williams—he's the one that just up and disappeared—I suspect Dodge wouldn't much cotton to the notion of playin' footsy with Earp."

"What're the odds on Earp making his peace with Brocius?"

"Well . . ." Slaughter said speculatively. "I reckon

anything's possible amongst cutthroats like them. But I'd say the odds are lots better that they're sittin' around figgerin' ways to bushwhack one another."

"What makes you think so?"

"Cause Brocius has a score to settle, what with Earp havin' killed three of his men. And Earp knows he ain't never gonna be safe till he's rid of Brocius. If for no other reason, I'd imagine he's damn tetchy about the fact that Brocius could tie him to those robberies."

There was a prolonged silence. Starbuck's gaze drifted to the fire, and he appeared lost in thought. At last, watching him closely, Slaughter shifted around in his chair.

"Where do you aim to start?"

Starbuck kneaded the back of his head. "Way it looks to me, I've got to get in thick with Earp. He's covered his tracks on the outside, so I'll have to worm my way on the inside. Sooner or later he'll slip, and when he does, I'll be there to get the goods on him."

"Sounds reasonable," Slaughter nodded gravely. "Course, I don't have to tell you, you'll be walkin' into a den of vipers. One miscue and they'll kill you deader'n hell."

"I'll play it close to the vest."

"That's the ticket!" Slaughter beamed. "And by Jesus, if you need any help, all you got to do is shout. I'd jump at the chance to tangle with them sorry bastards."

"Now that you mention it, I could use some advice."

"Anything a'tall! You name it."

"I need somebody to act as a go-between with Fred Dodge. Wouldn't do for me to be seen in his company, but I've got to funnel information through him to Wells, Fargo. Anybody come to mind?"

"Harry Woods," Slaughter informed him. "That's your man."

"The newspaper editor?" Starbuck looked skeptical. "I need somebody with a permanent case of lockjaw. You think he fits the bill?"

"Godalmightybingo!" Slaughter roared. "Harry hates Wyatt Earp worse'n the devil hates holy water. You couldn't find nobody better if you searched from now till doomsday."

Starbuck smiled, rising. "I'll take your word for it, and I'm obliged."

Slaughter argued persuasively, urging him to spend the night. But Starbuck had ridden almost a thousand miles, and he was anxious now to begin the hunt. As the sun neared its midday zenith, he stepped into the saddle and rode north toward Tombstone.

In early 1878 a bedraggled, footsore prospector struggled along the jagged mountain slopes east of San Pedro Valley. His name was Ed Schieffelin, and quite literally, he stumbled upon one of the richest silver strikes in frontier history. With ore assaying at twenty thousand dollars a ton, the discovery sparked the greatest mining boom ever recorded in the southwest. Schieffelin named his strike Tombstone, and within a matter of months, the mile-high camp had mushroomed into a carnival of speculation. A stagecoach line was established across the seventy-mile stretch of desert to Tucson. Men and machinery began pouring in, followed closely by merchants and tradesmen, gamblers and saloonkeepers, and the finest assemblage of whores ever gathered in the Arizona barrens. From a few hundred whiskery desert rats, huddled in tents and squalid shacks, Tombstone burst upon the map as a rip-roaring boomtown. Within three years, the population leaped to six thousand, and still growing. A town, complete with all the civilized vices, was spawned in a land previously thought inhabitable only by Apaches and scorpions. It was a dusty helldorado, vitalized by the motherlode, and it ran wide-open day and night.

Starbuck left his horse at the livery stable early next evening. Dusk was settling over Tombstone, and he had no trouble losing himself in the crowds of miners thronging the streets. While it was approaching suppertime, saloons and gaming parlors were already doing a brisk business.

Within a half hour he had located the *Nugget* office. Outside a saloon, directly across the street, he positioned himself where he could keep a watch on it. His grimy trail clothes and bearded stubble made him all but invisible among the grubby miners. On his fourth cigarette, the wait ended. A man he assessed as the printer stepped out the front door and hurried down the street. Only moments later, another man pulled the shades on the office windows.

Grinding his cigarette underfoot, he crossed the street and entered an alleyway beside the newspaper. He located the back door and rapped softly. From inside, he heard the sound of footsteps, then the door opened in a spill of light. The man who had pulled the windowshades stood framed in the doorway.

"Harry Woods?"

"Yes?"

"I have a message from John Slaughter."

"Slaughter?" Woods appeared confused, then quickly stepped aside. "Come in, Mr.—"

Starbuck entered, waiting until Woods shut the door. "The name's Starbuck. Luke Starbuck."

"Are you one of Slaughter's men?"

"Not exactly." Starbuck inspected the shop, satisfying himself they were alone. "I need some help, and Slaughter said you could be trusted."

Woods was a gnome of a man, with hair receding into a widow's peak and inquisitive eyes magnified behind thick glasses. He was slender and quick, highly intelligent, and grasped immediately the secretive nature of his visitor. He indicated the front office.

"Come this way."

Starbuck had reconciled himself to the risks involved in revealing his identity. Seated in the office, with Woods attentive and openly curious, he wasted no time in sparring around. He briefly described his mission for Wells, Fargo, stressing the fact that he would be operating undercover. Then he related everything Slaughter had told him regarding Wyatt Earp and Tombstone's volatile political climate. He concluded by asking the editor to act as a go-between with Fred Dodge. Woods, visibly caught up in the intrigue, agreed without hesitation.

"One other thing," Starbuck added. "I'll be operating under the name of Jack Johnson. Unless it's an emergency, don't even think of contacting me. One way or another, I'll manage to stay in touch with you."

"Anything else?" Woods asked. "Anything at all. I'm willing to go the limit if it'll rid Tombstone of Earp and his crowd."

"What about Earp?" Starbuck responded. "You got anything personal on him? Habits, family, that sort of thing."

"I do indeed!" Woods laughed. "I wrote an editor friend in Kansas, and asked him to check out the newspaper files. What he turned up was enlightening, to say the least."

"Such as?"

"Oh, the fact that the Earps got their start operating a two-bit whorehouse. Court records in Wichita prove it beyond a doubt."

"I'll be damned!"

"Moreover, Wyatt and two of his brothers married some of their former whores. That too is substantiated by court records."

Starbuck appeared puzzled. "I always understood Earp was a lawman in Kansas. How does that square with what you say?"

"He was an ordinary policeman," Woods countered. "He brags about being city marshal, but that's pure tommyrot. As a matter of fact, he was fired from the Wichita police force and all but run out of town. His record in Dodge City was somewhat better, but not much. He's a four-flusher and a liar, all puff and no substance."

Starbuck decided to reserve judgment. Earp appar-

ently resorted to violence and gunplay when necessary, and that hardly indicated a man without substance. "What about his family? You mentioned wives
a minute ago."

"Sluts!" Woods invested the word with scorn.
"Common trash, and no better than the men they married." He paused, thoughtful. "Earp's sister-in-law
might be the one exception. Her name is Alice Blaylock, and from what I've seen, she's a cut above the
rest."

"She's not married?"

Woods shook his head. "She lives with Earp and
his wife. All the brothers have houses nearby, over at
the west end of Fremont Street."

Starbuck pondered a moment. "Slaughter said Earp
operates a faro game at the Alhambra. Is that it . . . no
other business interests?"

"I've heard rumors that he's involved with some of
the big mining muckamucks. Of course, considering
he's such a grifter, he might have started the rumor
himself."

"Could you nose around, see what you can turn
up?"

"Glad to." Woods hesitated, studying him closely.
"If you don't mind my asking, how do you intend to
approach Earp?"

Starbuck smiled. "I'm a pretty fair gambler myself.
Figured I'd meet him on common ground and see
where it leads."

Several minutes elapsed while they discussed
Tombstone's sporting crowd. With some revealing in-
sights into the town and its shadier element, Starbuck

finally rose to leave. Woods recommended the Occidental Hotel, commenting that the food was passable and the clientele relatively civilized for a boomtown. At the door, Woods smiled warmly, offering his hand.

"Good hunting, Luke. And a Merry Christmas."

"Christmas?"

"Why, yes." Woods gave him a quizzical look. "Tonight's Christmas Eve."

"Yeah?" Starbuck seemed somehow surprised. "Well the same to you, Harry! Hope Ol' Nick leaves you something special."

Starbuck stepped into the alley, and Woods slowly closed the door. His excitement, the sense of intrigue and danger, suddenly gave way to an infinite sadness. He thought it somehow sorrowful that anyone could lose track of Christmas. Luke Starbuck seemed to him the loneliest man he'd ever met. Lonely, and very much alone.

CHAPTER 3

Christmas Day was bleak and chilly.

Mayor John Clum trudged down Fremont Street shortly after the noon hour. His expression was distracted, and he walked with the stoop-shouldered gait of one who bears a heavy burden. Only when he met passersby was he able to present his normal air of bonhomie. Then, exchanging holiday greetings, he tipped his hat and gave them a politician's smile. The effect was forced but nonetheless convincing.

At Fremont and First, he crossed to the southwest corner. There he mounted the stairs of a modest clapboard house. A coat of whitewash had turned the color of ancient ivory, and there was a look of general disrepair about the building. On the porch, the planks underfoot creaked like a coffin lid, and he suddenly dreaded the next few minutes. Then, halting before the door, he collected himself and knocked.

A moment later the door swung open. He doffed his hat and managed a weak grin. "Afternoon, Wyatt."

With a curt nod, Earp motioned him inside. "Out makin' the rounds, are you, John?"

"I was," Clum said, moving through the door. "Until I stopped off for a drink at the Oriental."

"Yeah?" Earp closed the door and turned to face him. "Something happen to change your plans?"

"I heard something that put the damper on my Christmas spirit. Thought you ought to hear it, too."

Clum dropped into a chair, and Earp took a seat across from him. Even in repose there was something sinister about Earp. He was of medium height, powerfully built, with close-cropped hair and a brushy handle-bar mustache. His slate-colored eyes and taciturn manner were striking, yet somehow cold and dispassionate. John Clum knew him to be a man who seemed impervious to even the simplest emotion.

"From the look on your face," Earp noted dryly, "you must've heard Santy Claus died."

There was an odor of fear about Clum. His composure, already strained, suddenly deserted him. Under Earp's level gaze, his voice was shaky and his features pallid.

"You remember Dave Parker?"

"The mining engineer?"

Clum nodded. "He laid over in Benson last night. Walked into a saloon and there was Curly Bill Brocius, big as life."

Earp's face grew overcast. "Alone?"

"Ringo and some of the others were with him. Parker said he was drunk as a lord, and not even Ringo could get him to keep his mouth shut."

"About what?"

"A death list," Clum said hesitantly. "He's drawn up a death list, Wyatt. Our names are right at the top, followed by Doc and your brothers and Judge Spicer."

"That a fact?" Earp asked, open scorn in his eyes. "And the minute you heard it, you come runnin' over here like your pants was on fire."

Clum hunched forward in his chair. "I'm serious, Wyatt. Parker was right there, heard it himself."

"Maybe so," Earp said crossly. "But it's a barroom brag, whiskey talk! Nothin' to it."

"You don't understand. He had an actual list! All our names down on paper! Parker said he was waving it around, and telling everyone within earshot how we were as good as dead. To me, that sounds like Brocius talking, not whiskey."

"You're easy spooked, aren't you, John?"

Clum was a squat, fat man with sagging cheeks and heavy jowls. He lived by his wits, and because of his glib way with words, he had achieved some small success both as a newspaper editor and a politician. But he abhorred violence, and possessed almost nothing in the way of physical courage. His own fear repulsed him, and with increasing frequency, he damned himself for allowing Earp to dominate his life. Today, however, he mustered one last spark of defiance.

"I'm thinking of selling the newspaper."

"Whatever gave you a damnfool notion like that?"

"Bill Brocius," Clum confessed. "Or at least he tipped the scales. I've been considering it for some time."

"Not thinkin' of leaving Tombstone, are you?"

"Yes, I am," Clum muttered, lowering his eyes. "The Indian Agent resigned over at the San Carlos Reservation. I had an idea I might apply for the job."

"You'd have to pull some strings, wouldn't you?"

"I've still got a few connections left."

Earp rose from his chair. He stuffed his hands in his pockets and stumped to the window. He stood looking down Fremont Street toward the center of town. But his eyes were fixed upon distance, and events.

In the main, Earp relied on the flaws and frailties of other men. He was ambitious and bold, and he believed that the weakness of others forever gave him an edge. Once, in a rare moment of candor, he had remarked, "There's only two kinds of people in this world. Them that takes and them that gets took." He had lived the better part of his life by that very code. He used people to his own ends, and then discarded them.

Yet his lodestone was not power alone. It was, instead, the fruits of power. He craved respect, and he was obsessed with the need for respectability. In the cowtowns of Kansas, he had lost the struggle to achieve that goal. His brothers were notorious as whoremongers, and he himself had never risen above the status of common policeman. Uprooting the entire family, he had traveled to Tombstone, searching for a fresh start. From the onset, nothing had gone as planned, and the killings at the OK Corral had further undercut his position. Still, for all his business and political setbacks, he wasn't yet willing to call it quits in Tombstone. Nor was he ready to discard John Clum.

At length, he turned from the window. His face congealed into a scowl, and his tone was hard. "I don't

like that idea, John. I want you to stick with the newspaper till I say different."

"To what purpose?"

"The purpose we had in mind from the start. Behan
and his crowd have got the upper hand right now, but
that'll change. One way or another, I still intend to get
control of the county."

Clum shook his head doubtfully. "Wyatt, we're
through in Tombstone and we're through in Cochise
County. I saw the handwriting on the wall when the
town council overrode me and fired Virge as marshal.
I stuck by you, but now"—he faltered, toying nervously with his hat—"Brocius means to kill us, and I
haven't got the stomach for it. I just want out."

Earp dismissed his objection with a brusque gesture. "You keep thinkin' like that and you'll be
scratchin' a poor man's ass all your life."

"Better a poor man than a dead man, and that seems
to me the only choice."

"Well, by God, it's not your choice to make!
You're gutless but you're not stupid. So get the wax
out of your ears and pay attention."

Clum looked ill. "Are you threatening me, Wyatt?"

With an unpleasant grunt, Earp crossed the parlor
and resumed his chair. "I'm tellin' you I need the
mayor's office to back my play, and I need that newspaper to influence public opinion. Like it or not, that
means I need you. So let's don't hear no more talk
about you hightailin' it out of town. Savvy?"

"What happens when you don't need me any
longer?"

"Aww for chrissake!" Earp groaned. "Stop worryin'

so much. We're all gonna come out of this rich as Midas."

"I hope you're not talking about stagecoaches."

"You just tend to your knittin' and let me handle the details."

"Wyatt, listen to me, please! We can't afford any more trouble. One mistake and we'll all wind up in prison . . . or worse."

"There you go again, borrowing trouble."

"I'm simply stating a fact. Behan is watching us like a hawk, and Brocius has put our names on a death list. Good God, we're in too deep already! Why dig the hole any deeper?"

"The only holes I mean to dig are the kind with headstones. One for Brocius, and maybe even one for Behan—unless he stays clear of my business."

"No more," Clum pleaded. "I have nightmares about it, Wyatt."

"Nightmares about what?"

"Marsh Williams," Clum said hollowly. "There was no need . . . you shouldn't have—"

"Close your trap!" Earp glowered at him, motioning toward the kitchen. "The women are in there, so button up and stay buttoned up."

"Sorry. I guess I wasn't thinking."

Anger flashed in Earp's eyes, then his gaze narrowed and his look became veiled. "Don't lose your nerve on me, John. You might recall that's why Marsh Williams—disappeared."

"I know," Clum said in a resigned voice. "It won't happen again. You can depend on me, Wyatt."

"Never thought otherwise. Now, since you're here, let's talk a little business."

Earp leaned forward, elbows on his knees. The timbre of his voice dropped, and he began speaking in measured tones. John Clum listened, nodding attentively, all the while gripped by a numbing thought. He wondered if he would ever leave Tombstone alive.

In the kitchen, Alice Blaylock tried to close her mind to the drone of voices from the parlor. She had heard Earp's sudden outburst, and sensed that the mayor's visit had put her brother-in-law in one of his foul moods. Any hope for a pleasant Christmas dinner was now lost forever.

She was seated at a work table, peeling potatoes. Her sister, Mattie, stood at the sink, washing dishes left over from a late breakfast. The heat from an iron woodrange kept the kitchen toasty warm. A plump hen, already stuffed and in the oven, flooded the room with a savory aroma. It was, Alice told herself, the best of all times in the Earp household. A tranquil interlude, performing domestic chores, when she and Mattie could pretend the outside world didn't exist. Yet she knew it was only that—an interlude.

She glanced at Mattie, and a deep feeling of pity washed over her. Once attractive, Mattie was now worn and frail. Her complexion was prematurely lined by too many years in the harsh western climate. Her eyes, wrinkled at the corners by crows' feet, bore a perpetually worried expression. On her face were stamped the ravages of a cruel and unmerciful life. She was thirty years old, and looked at least forty.

Alice, who was four years younger, sometimes felt guilty about her own looks. Her black hair was drawn sleekly to the nape of her neck, accentuating the smooth contours of her face and the healthy glow of youth. Her eyes were dark and expressive, and she had a sunny, vivacious smile. She wasn't tall, but she carried herself well, dressing to compliment her slender figure. The overall effect was disarming and somehow provocative. A curious blend of innocence and minx-like worldliness.

Appearances aside, few people suspected that she was indeed an innocent. By contrast, the women of the Earp family were inured to the harsher realities of life. She had learned, much to her dismay, that vice had been their livelihood, almost a family enterprise. At times, she still had difficulty reconciling herself to the fact that Mattie was a retired prostitute.

A year ago, never once suspicioning the truth, she had come West to join her sister. Their parents, killed that spring in one of Ohio's perennial floods, had left her with meager resources. She had several suitors, hometown boys who bored her to distraction, and she briefly entertained the idea of marriage. But wedding a man for security rather than love was foreign to her character. Filled with romantic notions about the frontier, she had entrained for Arizona Territory.

Once in Tombstone, her schoolgirl illusions were quickly disabused. She found life in the mining camp coarse and uncivilized, with none of the colorful adventure she'd read about in dime novels. But her greatest letdown by far was Mattie's husband. She discovered her sister had married a monster.

By stages, a word here and a word there, she gradually learned the whole truth. Mattie, traveling the Kansas cowtowns with a troupe of entertainers, had been stranded in Wichita. Fallen on hard times, she was befriended by the Earps and lured into a life of prostitution. A year or so later, when the family departed for Dodge City, she went along as Wyatt's woman. Then, shortly before the move to Tombstone, they were married. Wyatt needed a wife to help him create a respectable front, and Mattie saw him as her last chance to outdistance the cowtowns. It was calculated and mutually advantageous. An arrangement.

Over the past year, Alice had learned all this and more. At first appalled, she slowly came to understand Mattie's reasons, and with understanding came acceptance. To her sorrow, she also came to understand that Wyatt Earp was, by nature, an insensitive brute. He was devoid of compassion, and in the privacy of his home, he sometimes displayed a sadistic streak. All the worse, he was corrupt and conniving, unscrupulous with anyone outside the immediate family. The killings last October—three men callously gunned down at the OK Corral—had left her chilled to the very marrow. She knew virtually nothing of death, and found it all but incomprehensible that she lived under the same roof with a killer. There was a sense of terror and unreality about it. The terror of awakening from a bad dream—and finding it true.

Insofar as her personal life was concerned, it had simply ceased to exist. The Earps were pariahs, and their women were the stuff of vicious gossip. In Tombstone, no decent man would tip his hat to an

Earp woman, much less pay her court or invite her to
a social. Apart from Doc Holliday, and Wyatt's business cronies, few men ever came to the house anyway.
She had no opportunity of meeting anyone worth-
while, and even less chance of being accepted by the
respectable members of the community. Her name was
Blaylock, and she'd done nothing to deserve censure.
But to the townspeople, she was nonetheless one of
the Earp women.

Alice often wondered how she had allowed herself
to become trapped. Her own naivete was certainly one
element, and her love and concern for Mattie was another. Yet she recognized all that as being more excuse
than justification. On days like today, when she
dwelled on it at any length, the situation seemed particularly noxious. Unless she was careful, she slipped
into fits of self-loathing, and bitter regret. She searched
for the strength to walk out the front door and never
look back. Then, struck by the fact that she had no
money and no prospects, she was reminded of a
greater fear. Fallen on hard times, stranded in a remote
mining camp, she too might resort to that older pro-
fession. The thought left her queasy, and desperate.

Mattie's voice intruded on her trancelike lapse. She
suddenly realized she was sitting with the knife in one
hand and a potato in the other, and staring blankly at
the tabletop. She looked up and found Mattie watching
her with a puzzled frown.

"I'm sorry," she said lightly. "I must have been
star-gazing."

"We all do, honeybun. It's about the only form of
entertainment the womenfolk in this family ever get."

"Did you ask me something?"

"After a fashion," Mattie observed, nodding toward the parlor. "When Wyatt and the mayor get through, I want you to be careful what you say."

"What would I say?"

"The less the better. And most especially, don't let on that we overheard what they were talking about."

Alice shuddered. "I overheard nothing. Absolutely nothing."

Mattie drew a deep, unsteady breath. "I'd give the world to say the same. Sometimes it's more than a body can stand."

"I know," Alice said darkly. "Every night I pray it just doesn't get any worse. Surely it won't, not after all this time."

"Oh Lordy!" Mattie said in a musing voice. "How I wish we'd never come to this town. I'd gladly kick it over and go back to Kansas."

"No, don't say—"

Alice stopped, glancing quickly toward the parlor. The men's voices were louder now, and the creak of floorboards filtered through the house. A few moments later the front door closed, and everything went still. Then the sound of footsteps became apparent, a measured tread growing closer. Alice began peeling potatoes, and Mattie grabbed the pump handle, jacking a rush of water into the sink. Neither of them gave any indication they heard the approaching steps.

Earp halted in the doorway. "When the hell we gonna eat? I've got business uptown."

"Damnit, Wyatt!" Mattie whirled around, hands on

her hips. "Won't your business keep till another time? It's Christmas!"

"So what?" Earp said sourly. "It's also a big gaming night, and in case you forgot, I'm a dealer."

"Well, I'd think you could take the night off. Especially Christmas night!"

"Just get it on the table and don't argue about it."

Earp turned and stalked back into the parlor. Mattie waited, listening until he had moved out of earshot. Then she winked at Alice and lowered her voice in conspiratorial whisper.

"We'll have our own Christmas! Just like old times, when we was kids and people still laughed."

"Yes." Alice smiled sadly. "Just like old times."

CHAPTER 4

Starbuck went undercover that night.

Around eight o'clock he eased through the door of the Alhambra. He was tricked out in a black broadcloth jacket, set off by a white linen shirt and a fancy string tie. On his head, cocked at a rakish angle, was a slouch hat, and on his feet he wore kidskin halfboots polished to a dazzling luster. A blind man would have spotted him as a professional gambler.

The Alhambra was one of Tombstone's finer gaming establishments. A mahogany bar ran the length of one wall. Behind it was a gaudy clutch of bottles with a gleaming mirror flanked by ubiquitous nude paintings. Along the opposite wall were keno and faro layouts, a roulette table, and a chuck-a-luck game. At the far end of the room were the poker tables, their baize covers muted by the cider glow of low-hanging lamps. The atmosphere was cordial and restrained, devoted solely to the pursuit of chance.

Halting at the bar, Starbuck ordered whiskey. After a couple of sips, he hooked one elbow over the counter and turned to survey the room. The crowd, much as he'd expected, was a mixed lot. Tradesmen and drummers, spiffy in their townclothes, were ganged around the tables with miners and cowhands and rough-garbed teamsters. The action was fast and without pause, broken only by a low murmur of conversation and winner-loser calls by the housemen. To all appearances, the games were honest, relying on house odds to turn a profit. The amount of money exchanging hands indicated the Alhambra was doing very well indeed.

Starbuck's inspection was casual but nonetheless exact. He spotted Earp at the faro layout and examined him with the fleeting curiosity of a fellow craftsman. His gaze drifted then to the back of the room, searching for Doc Holliday. From what Harry Woods, the newspaper editor, had told him, Holliday was an inveterate poker player and a man of distinctive appearance. The information was accurate on both counts. With no trouble, Starbuck located Holliday at the center table. Another glance confirmed that every chair at all three tables was occupied.

Turning to the bar, he took out a silver cigar case and selected a thin black cheroot. He struck a match, lighting the cheroot, aware of its strange acrid taste. As part of his disguise, he had chosen cigars over roll-your-owns, which was more in keeping with the image of a natty high-roller. He stuck the cheroot in the corner of his mouth, and stood for a moment reviewing the plan he'd decided upon earlier. He saw no reason to alter it now, for the physical layout of the Alhambra dovetailed perfectly with what he had in mind. He finished his drink and dropped a cartwheel on the counter.

Threading his way through the crowd, he walked toward the rear of the room. Several onlookers were clustered around the poker tables, and he casually moved through their ranks. Presently, after a brief inspection of each game, he took up a position near the center table. There were seven players, and it appeared to be a high stakes game. Out of the corner of his eye, he slowly scrutinized Doc Holliday. He was struck by the thought that here was a mankiller who looked the part.

Holliday was a tall, emaciated man, with ash-blond hair and a drooping mustache. Somewhere in his thirties, his visage was that of an undertaker; sober but not really sad. He wore a swallowtail coat and a black cravat, with a gold watch chain looped across his vest. His attitude toward the other players was an inimical union of gruff sufferance and thinly disguised contempt. Speculation had it that he had killed twenty-six men, and his manner left no question that he was equal to the task. He impressed Starbuck as someone who could walk into an empty room and start a fight.

The game was dealer's choice, restricted to stud poker and five card draw. Ante was twenty dollars, with a fifty dollar limit and three raises. Check and raise was permitted, which meant it was a cutthroat game, attracting players who took their poker seriously. The rules seemed tailor-made to Starbuck's scheme. All he had to do, he told himself, was somehow manage to beat Holliday.

That promised to be an uphill challenge. The former

dentist was a skilled gambler. He won on what appeared to be weak hands, and evidenced an uncanny knack for reading the other players. There was no pattern to his betting and raising; his erratic play made him unpredictable, and somewhat intimidating. He would bluff on a bad hand as often as he folded, and more often than not his bluff went undetected. On good hands, he would sometimes raise forcefully, allowing the money to speak for itself. At other times, when he held good cards, he would lay back and sucker his opponents into heedless raises. He was by far the best player at the table, and he won steadily.

Perhaps a half hour went past before one of the players quit the game. Starbuck jockeyed himself into position even as the man rose from his chair. Nodding around the table, he seated himself and smiled broadly. He pulled a thick wad of greenbacks from his pocket and made a show of stacking them neatly before him. Then he settled back in his chair and gave the other players a look of amiable bravado.

"Jack Johnson, at your service, gents."

Every eye at the table was on him, but no one spoke. Across from him, Holliday gathered the cards, riffled them expertly, and began dealing stud. Starbuck caught aces back to back on the first two cards, and checked. Then, on the third card, he began betting. Three players tried to draw out on him, but the aces held. He won an easy five hundred on the first hand.

Over the years, Starbuck had become something of an actor. His undercover work, by necessity, dictated that he assume various roles and disguises. Tonight, he was acting the part of a convivial smoothtalker. He

was gregarious, outwardly charming, and presented
himself as an affable jokester. He pulled it off with a
certain panache, and he was utterly convincing. He
was also lucky.

For the next few hours, the cards fell his way with
consistent regularity. He won on small pairs, weak
straights, and an occasional flush. More than his own
luck, it seemed that fortune had deserted the other
players. He was winning with hands that normally
would have taken second place, and no pots. Yet, for
all his luck, he was careful to establish a pattern. When
he bluffed, he made a point of backing his play with
unusually large bets. He used the ploy infrequently,
but with jocular skill. Several times he was aware that
Holliday was covertly studying him. With the trap
baited, he awaited the right moment.

His chance came in the third hour of play. He
opened a hand of five card draw with a fifty dollar bet.
Everyone dropped out except Holliday, and he raised.
Starbuck bumped it the limit and Holliday took the
third raise. On the draw, Holliday took three cards and
Starbuck stood pat. After another round of betting and
raising, Holliday laid down two pair. Starbuck chuckled, spreading out three of a kind, and raked in the
pot. He caught a tiny glint of surprise in Holliday's
eyes.

A few hands later he again seized opportunity. The
game was stud poker. With three cards dealt, he had
a pair of tens showing, and bet fifty dollars. Holliday
obviously couldn't believe he would try the same gambit twice running, and tested with a raise. Starbuck
merely called, and checked the bet on the fourth card.

But on the fifth card he again bet the limit. Holliday raised, certain now he was bluffing. He bumped it fifty and waited, puffing on his cheroot. Holliday watched him narrowly a moment, then called. He flipped his hole card, revealing a third ten.

"Three tens wins! Better luck next time, mister."

Holiday grunted coarsely. "I got to admire your style, Johnson. That's twice you sandbagged me."

"Well, sir, I'd say twice is plenty for one night. I thank you kindly."

Starbuck stood, pocketing a considerably larger roll of greenbacks. He scooped up a handful of gold coins and nodded cheerily to the other players. Then he turned to leave.

Holliday fixed him with a querulous squint. "Some folks think it's not polite to win and run."

Starbuck mugged, hands outstretched. "No offense intended, but there's the other side of the coin. Some folks never learn to quit when they're ahead."

Holliday coughed, wheezing hoarsely, and pulled a handkerchief from inside his coat pocket. He covered his mouth, waiting until the wheezing subsided, then raked Starbuck with a cold glare. "A sporting man would give the losers a chance to recoup a bit before he ducks out."

"Glad to oblige!" Starbuck gave him a nutcracker grin, and clamped the cheroot between his teeth. "Another day, another time—but not tonight!"

Bowing, he flipped Holliday an offhand salute and walked away. Behind him there was a pall of silence, and he noticed some of the onlookers watching him with odd looks of disbelief. Clearly, no one had ever gaffed Holiday and lived to tell the tale. He thought he'd pulled it off rather neatly.

Drifting back to the bar, he took up a position directly in front of the mirror. He felt reasonably confident Holliday wouldn't push the matter further. Still, there were no guarantees, and he'd learned never to take undue chances with known gunmen. After ordering a drink, he leaned into the bar, casually dropping his right hand below counter level. He was now carrying the Colt in a crossdraw holster, and the butt was within an inch of his fingertips. The wide backbar mirror gave him a view of the entire room. With one eye on Holliday, he was also able to observe Wyatt Earp at work.

Faro was one of the more popular games in western cowtowns and mining camps. Its name derived from the image of an Egyptian pharaoh on the back of the cards, and the game had originated a century earlier in France.

Cards were dealt from a specially adapted box, and the player bet against the house. Every card from ace to king was painted on the cloth layout that covered the table. A player placed his money on the card of his choice, and two cards were then drawn face up from the box. The first card drawn lost and the second card won. The player could "copper" his play by betting a card to lose instead of win. There were twenty-five turns, since the first and last cards in the deck paid nothing. When the box was empty, the dealer shuffled and the game began anew.

Normally, the house hired an experienced gambler to operate the game. The dealer worked for a salary, plus a small share of the winnings. Sometimes, when a gambler had developed a reputation and a following, the house leased him the concession. Through Harry Woods, Starbuck had learned that this was the arrangement between Earp and the Alhambra. The game was Earp's and he backed the faro bank with his own money. The house received a weekly payment for the concession, plus a percentage of the winnings. With luck, and a knowledge of human nature, a faro operator could earn a handsome living. Which was one of the things that bothered Starbuck.

A handsome living hardly seemed sufficient for a man of Earp's demonstrated ambition. His activities in Tombstone left no doubt that he had raised his sights to a larger game, and much higher stakes. So far he had failed, but he was obviously undeterred. Otherwise he would have cut his losses and gone off in search of riper opportunity. The faro game, then, was merely a front. Wyatt Earp stayed on in Tombstone for reasons as yet unrevealed. Once uncovered, those reasons might very well provide the key to robbery and murder. And put a rope around Earp's neck.

Some while later, Starbuck noted a lull at the faro layout. The last player, clearly a loser, walked away and left Earp alone at the table. It was the opening Starbuck had waited for, and time to put the second stage of his plan into operation. He steeled himself to play it fast and loose—and act the part.

With a sauntering step, he moved across the room. The expression on his face was peacock proud, the look of a gambler who had found his mark for the night and scored well. He halted before the table, smiling pleasantly.

"How's tricks?"

"Tolerable." Earp's eyes were impersonal. "Care to try your luck?"

"Yessir, I do!" Starbuck said carelessly. "Got a sudden urge to buck the tiger."

"Get a hunch, bet a bunch."

Earp deftly shuffled the cards and allowed Starbuck to cut. Then he placed the deck in the dealing box and burned the top card, commonly referred to as the "soda" card. Glancing up, he nodded, indicating the game was open to play. Starbuck dug out his handful of gold coins, placing one above the ace, another between the five-six, and still another between the jack-queen. By playing several cards at once, he immediately marked himself as a professional. The system was known as "coppering the heel," and increased the chances of winning. Earp pulled two cards from the box, a king and a four.

"Close," he said in the slick cadence of a pitchman. "Give 'er another go."

"Keep dealing!" Starbuck laughed, scattering coins across the layout. "I'm on a streak tonight."

Earp was adroit and quick. His hands flashed between the box and the layout with practiced expertise. Cards popped out of the box in speedy pairs, and just as rapidly he paid the winners and collected the losers. Starbuck continued to "copper the heel," but for every bet he won, he lost double and sometimes more. He blithely tossed coins about the layout, alternately chuckling and cursing with the gusto of a man who was enjoying himself immensely. Halfway through the deck, the last of his gold coins disappeared. By the time the "hoc" card, the last card in the deck, was turned, he was deep into his wad of greenbacks. Within a matter of minutes, Earp had trimmed him for something more than a thousand dollars.

"Seems like the worm's turned."

"Damned if it don't!"

"Maybe it's just as well," Earp remarked. "Doc don't tolerate people that quit winners. He'll likely simmer down now."

"Doc?"

"Doc Holliday." Earp nodded toward the poker tables. "The fellow you snookered a while ago."

"No kiddin'!" Starbuck's eyes widened in feigned astonishment. "*The* Doc Holliday?"

"The one and only."

"Well I'll be double-dipped! I sure hope there's no hard feelings. You reckon he's still sore?"

"Don't wory about it," Earp advised wryly. "Doc wouldn't monkey with a customer of mine."

"How's that?"

"You might say we're on a first name basis."

"Wait a minute—" Words appeared to fail Starbuck. "Your name wouldn't be ... are you Wyatt Earp?"

"Yeah, I generally answer to it."

"Judas Priest!" Starbuck grinned foolishly, and began pumping his arm. "I read all about you in the newspapers! That shootout you had with those desperadoes. It's an honor to meet you, Mr. Earp. Yessir, a puredee honor!"

Earp regarded him with impassive curiosity. "You new to Tombstone?"

"Pulled in last night," Starbuck said eagerly. "Name's Jack Johnson—my friends call me Jack."

"I take it you're a gamblin' man?"

"Poker's my game." Starbuck flicked an ash off his cheroot, and chuckled softly. "Course, I got a fatal weakness for faro. Keeps me busted most of the time."

"Johnson?" Earp eyed him thoughtfully. "Turkey Creek Jack Johnson?"

Starbuck had lifted the alias from a dead man. The risk was slight, with virtually no chance of exposure. But now, pretending wariness, he gave Earp a guarded look.

"What makes you ask?"

"Heard of you," Earp commented. "Deadwood, wasn't it?"

"You name it. Leadwood, Cripple Creek, Dead-wood. I've worked all the camps."

"I was in Deadwood once't."

"Oh, when was that?"

"Back in '76."

"Before or after Hicock was killed?"

"Few months before."

Starbuck wagged his head. "You should've been there. I wasn't standing ten feet away when Jack McCall drilled him through the head."

"You saw him get it?"

"Doggone right!" Starbuck puffed importantly on his cheroot. "Saw it with my very own eyes!"

"I heard tell," Earp said in a voice without tone,

"he was holdin' aces and nines when he got it. Any truth to that?"

Starbuck sensed he was being tested. The reason was unclear, but he played along with a straightface. "You must've heard wrong. It was aces and eights. Goddamn cards had to be pried out of his hand."

"Likely you're right," Earp agreed idly. "What brings you to Tombstone?"

"Well—" Starbuck hesitated, then smiled cryptically. "You might say I came south for my health."

"Lots of folks do." Earp appeared to lose interest, indicating the layout. "Care to give it another try?"

"Not tonight!" Starbuck laughed. "I'll have to find me a poker game just to break even."

"Do yourself a favor and gaff somebody besides Doc. I'd like to keep you as a regular customer."

"Damn good advice." Starbuck bobbed his head, grinning. "See you next time I'm flush."

"Anytime, Jack. You're always welcome at my table."

Walking away, Starbuck silently congratulated himself. The next step would be easier. And the one after that, easier still.

CHAPTER 5

Early the next afternoon, Starbuck went for a stroll. Other than the hotel and the Alhambra, he'd seen little of the town since arriving. Like a wolf prowling new territory, he always felt more comfortable once he had his bearings. He reminded himself to avoid the Wells, Fargo office and the *Nugget*. Those were places to be visited only after dark.

Upon leaving the hotel, he walked west on Allen Street. Tombstone was laid out in a grid pattern, with the business district centralized in the heart of town. The main thoroughfares were Allen Street and Fremont Street, both crossing the grid east to west. North and west of downtown were the better residential areas. To the south were warehouses and the less desirable residential quarter. Vice, in the form of cribs and parlor houses, was restricted to the eastern section of the community.

Allen Street boasted most of the saloons and gambling establishments, along with three additional hotels and the Birdcage Theatre. One block north, on Fremont Street, was the main commercial district. City

Hall and a couple of banks were flanked by several blocks of cafes, shops, and general business concerns. At night, when Tombstone's sporting element awakened, Allen Street came alive. But during the day, Fremont Street was the busiest part of town. Here the hustle and bustle of everyday affairs was conducted in a more sedate atmosphere.

Starbuck was in no hurry, and he criss-crossed the town at a leisurely pace. As he walked, he gained a better perspective into Wyatt Earp's motives. Tombstone, by light of day, revealed itself as a veritable money tree. The outlying mines were processing millions of dollars of silver every year. Unlike most mining camps, the influx of people and a stable economy had created a sense of permanence. Whoever controlled the political apparatus of Cochise County would have access to a fortune in graft and taxes. Whoever wore the sheriff's badge would play a key role in the distribution of that largesse. Moreover, the sheriff's office would provide a legitimate front for other, less acceptable, forms of skullduggery. It was small wonder that Earp had twice sought the post of the county's chief lawman.

Had Earp been elected, the tin star would have made him all but invulnerable. Starbuck saw that even more clearly now; there would have been no way to infiltrate the ranks of a crooked sheriff and his henchmen. Yet a common gambler—not to mention a social leper—was an altogether different matter. Starbuck had only to prove that he and Earp were birds of a feather. He could then progress to a chummier relationship, and invent some device to make himself valuable. From there, it would require only time and guile until he wormed his way into Earp's confidence. A similar dodge had worked with all manner of horse thieves and cattle rustlers. And he had every confidence it would work with an overly ambitious faro dealer.

Around midafternoon Starbuck paused at the corner of Fifth and Fremont. His gaze fell on a general emporium, and he recalled he was almost out of cigars. He entered the store, and moved directly to the counter. A clerk hurried forward.

"Yessir, what can we do for you today?"

"Need a box of cheroots."

"Any special brand?"

"You got Varga's Deluxe?"

"Yes, indeedy." The clerk turned toward the shelves, calling back over his shoulder. "Take your time, Miss Blaylock. I'll only be a moment."

The name struck a chord. Starbuck glanced around and saw a girl one aisle over, inspecting yardgoods. She was small and compactly built, with attractive oval features. A woolen shawl was draped across her shoulders, and curls the color of sable were visible beneath her bonnet. He thought to himself she was easy on the eyes. Not a beauty, but close enough to draw second looks.

Then the name clicked, and he instantly made the connection. Harry Woods had mentioned Earp's sister-in-law. *Alice Blaylock.* And it hardly seemed possible there would be two Miss Blaylocks in a town the size of Tombstone. He felt reasonably certain this was the girl.

Before he could think it through, the clerk returned with his cigars. He paid, waiting for his change, all the while weighing the possibilities. Nothing workable occurred to him, but he resolved somehow to make her acquaintance. According to Woods, she was the only single woman in the entire Earp family. That, in itself, presented a grab bag full of options.

Outside the store, he walked upstreet a short distance. He halted in front of a mercantile, playing for time, and made a production of lighting a cheroot. Here, he told himself, was a made-to-order opportunity. If he could get close to the girl, that might very well open the door to the Earp household. Which wouldn't exactly make him one of the family, but it would be a large step in the right direction. On top of that, he'd been known to charm a few girls out of their undies and leave them begging for more. With a little romance and sweet-talk, he might easily con her into spilling all the family secrets. Certainly, he had nothing to lose by trying. The only stickler was how to approach it. He couldn't let on that he knew her name, yet he had to manage it in some offhand manner. And quickly!

Out of the corner of his eye, he saw her leave the emporium and turn in his direction. She was carrying several bundles, wrapped in brown paper, and the distance was closing rapidly. With no time to plan it out, he simply reverted to the old standby.

Puffing on his cigar, he gave every appearance of being engrossed with the mercantile's window display. As she approached, he suddenly turned and bulled directly into her path. The collision rocked her back on her heels and sent her packages flying. She gave a little yelp of fright, clutching at her bonnet.

"Pardon me, ma'am!" Starbuck grabbed her arm, supporting her. "Are you all right?"

Alice Blaylock nodded, trying to collect herself. "Yes, I think so. At least nothing seems broken."

"I'm sure sorry!" Starbuck hurried on. "No excuse for it! You're so dainty and all, I might've hurt you bad."

"No, really," Alice assured him. "I'm perfectly fine."

"Well, it was awful clumsy of me all the same. You just catch your breath and let me tend to those bundles."

Starbuck quickly gathered her packages off the boardwalk, and stuck them under one arm. Almost as an afterthought, he took the cheroot from his mouth and tossed it into the street. Then he gave her a lop-sided grin, and tipped his hat.

"Jack Johnson, ma'am. And purely mortified to make your acquaintance like a runaway steam engine."

"No need to apologize, Mr. Johnson."

"Well now, that's mighty kind of you, Miss—?"

"Blaylock. Alice Blaylock."

"Miss Blaylock," Starbuck murmured pleasantly. "Here, let me carry these bundles for you aways. That's the least I can do, after nearly bowling you over."

Alice looked startled, on the verge of objecting. Then she seemed to change her mind. She smiled, turning uptown, and he fell in beside her.

"Are you new to Tombstone, Mr. Johnson?"

"I am, for a fact," Starbuck said genially. "How'd you guess?"

It was no guess. Every member of the Earp family was known on sight to the townspeople. Only a stranger would have failed to recognize her, and on sudden impulse, Alice found herself quite taken with him. He was courteous, with a certain rough charm, and rather good looking. Far and away the nicest thing that had happened to her since coming to Tombstone. She silently thanked her stars that he was indeed a stranger.

"I've lived here a while," she said casually. "I suppose you might say I'm one of Tombstone's old timers."

"Say now!" Starbuck's face split in a grin. "I reckon that makes it my lucky day."

"Oh, how so?"

"Because," Starbuck suggested, "you being familiar with the town, you might take pity on a stranger."

Alice blinked with surprise. "Excuse me?"

"I know it's bold as brass, but I was hoping you'd have dinner with me. I'd sure count it an honor, Miss Blaylock."

"Dinner?" Alice repeated the word as if she couldn't have heard correctly. "You're asking me out?"

"Yes, ma'am," Starbuck said smoothly. "I might never get another chance, and I wouldn't want to risk that."

"I—" Alice sounded uncertain. "I don't know."

"I'm a gentleman." Starbuck's square face was very earnest. "I don't take liberties with ladies, and you wouldn't have to worry a minute. You've got my word on it, and anybody will tell you—Jack Johnson's word is good as gold!"

Starbuck buttered her up all the way to the corner. By then, her head was spinning and she found herself completely captivated by his jocular manner. When they parted, he had directions to her house and an engagement for dinner. He tipped his hat, grinning, and strolled away. She felt slightly giddy, and dared not pinch herself.

Night was coming on as Starbuck approached the Earp house. To the west, under a darkening sky, low clouds scudded across the horizon. Out of habit, he tested the wind, then quickly set the thought aside. Tonight, he had only one concern, and it wasn't the weather.

Nor was it the girl. If anything, she had proved more gullible than he'd expected. She had fallen for his glib line and he felt she could be coaxed along very nicely. His major concern was Wyatt Earp. However innocent it appeared, he knew his chance meeting with the girl would draw suspicion. All afternoon he had schooled himself to give a sterling performance. Earp would be waiting when he entered the house, and at that instant, there would be no margin for error. He had to appear genuinely dumbfounded—flabbergasted!

Freshly shaved, and reeking of bayberry lotion, he mounted the porch stairs. Halting, he removed his hat and took a tight grip on his nerves. Then he knocked.

A few seconds later the door opened. Wyatt Earp, expressionless, stood framed in a glow of lamplight.

"Mr. Earp!" Starbuck gave him a walleyed look of amazement. "What are you doing here?"

"I live here."

"You—" Starbuck shook his head. "I thought this was the Blaylock house."

"C'mon in." Earp moved aside. "I'm married to Alice's sister."

"Well, I'll be damned!" Starbuck said with a dopey grin. "Don't that take the cake? You're kin!"

"After a fashion." Earp closed the door, turning to a man standing nearby. "Like you to meet one of my brothers. Virge, this here's Jack Johnson."

Virgil Earp was a lean man, with hard eyes and a slow smile. The family resemblance was immediately apparent, and like his brother, his upper lip was covered with a brushy mustache. He offered his hand to Starbuck and they shook once, a hard up-and-down pump.

"Pleased to meet you, Mr. Johnson."

"Jack," Starbuck said affably. "Folks call my pa Mr. Johnson."

"Wyatt tells me you're a gambler."

"That's my trade."

"Appears we've got lots in common, don't it?"

Starbuck played dumb. "We do?"

"Alice," Virge remarked. "First time she says boo to a stranger, and you turn out to be a gamblin' man."

"Well—" Starbuck darted a sheepish glance at Earp. "Look here, I hope there's no hard feelings about me asking her out. If I'd known she was related, I would've worked out a proper introduction. No two ways about it!"

"She's full grown," Earp informed him. "Treat her right, and you won't hear no complaints out of me."

"I appreciate it, Mr. Earp. That's mighty white of you."

"Why don't you forget that Mr. Earp stuff. The name's Wyatt."

Before Starbuck could reply, Alice entered from a hallway door. Her dress was navy serge, clearly the remnants of better days, and the same woolen shawl was thrown over her shoulders. But her hair was curled in elaborate finger-puffs and her eyes positively shone. She moved across the parlor with willowy grace.

"Good evening, Mr. Johnson."

"Ma'am." Starbuck faked a bemused smile. "I was just telling Mr. Earp—Wyatt—that I sure didn't mean any disrespect. I never had a glimmer you two was related."

"Fiddlesticks!" Alice flashed her brother-in-law a look. "He knows that very well."

Earp nodded solemnly. "I already told him he's welcome, Allie. Don't get yourself worked up."

Starbuck sensed an underlying tension, and suppressed a smile. Earp and the girl were clearly at odds, which fitted perfectly with his plan. He made a stab at polite conversation, but it went along in fits and starts, then petered out altogether. Finally, with Alice edging toward the door, he bid the Earp brothers goodnight. A wide grin plastered across his face, he waved and followed her into the night.

When the door closed, Virge muttered a low oath. "I don't like it."

"Your crystal ball workin' overtime, is it?"

"You asked me over here to size him up, and I'm tellin' you—he smells like trouble!"

"Maybe, maybe not," Earp allowed. "You didn't see his face when I opened the door. He goddamn near swallowed his tongue."

"C'mon, Wyatt," Virge scoffed. "You've conned too many people in your time to be taken in by that."

"Yeah, and I know the difference, too. I've got a hunch he's on the square."

"What happened to coincidence?" Virge reminded him. "Last night he sits down at your table out of the clear blue. Today he just accidently happens to bump into Allie on the street. You was the one that said it went against the odds."

"I've been wrong before," Earp said stubbornly. "I just don't think he could've fooled me. Nobody's that good an actor."

Virge's look was colored by skepticism. "Still seems awful damn peculiar he showed up so soon after Marsh Williams . . . disappeared."

"Soon?" Earp demanded. "Hell's fire, close to a month's passed. I don't call that soon."

"Confound it, Wyatt!" Virge said hotly. "What if he's a Wells, Fargo agent? You're stakin' a helluva lot on the fact that he didn't pee down his leg when you opened the door."

"Well, one thing's for certain," Earp said sardonically. "Whatever he is or isn't, he's got Allie in a halfway decent humor. I take my hat off to him for that."

"You're beggin' for trouble, Wyatt. And if you're not careful, you're liable to get it."

Earp frowned. "All right, if it'll ease your mind, sound him out the first chance you get. Turkey Creek Jack Johnson ought to know all there is to know about them northern mining camps."

"By God, don't worry! I'll do that very thing!"

Earp slumped down in a chair and crossed his legs. He smiled to himself, remembering the look on his sister-in-law's face. With time, and encouragement, Johnson might just take the little bitch off his hands. For good and forever.

On the walk downtown, Starbuck kept the conversation light and inconsequential. True to his word, he intended to treat her like a lady. And not a lady of negotiable virtue, like the other Earp women. Such a novelty would impress her, and bring her all the more quickly to his bed. Then the real work could commence.

With her hand tucked inside his arm, he continued to play the raffish charmer. "Did Wyatt tell you how I clipped Doc Holliday?"

"No," she said with a firmness that surprised him. "He didn't."

"Uh-oh!" Starbuck chuckled. "I hope you haven't got anything against gamblers. Wyatt must've told you that's how I make my living."

"Not gamblers," she confided, a spark of deviltry in her eyes. "Just Doc Holliday."

"Can you keep a secret?"

"Try me and see."

"I don't like him either," Starbuck said jokingly. "Never could stand a sore loser."

She cocked her head in a funny little smile. "Do you ever lose?"

"Now you're asking trade secrets."

"Tell me," she said brightly. "Do you?"

"Promise it won't go any further?"

"Cross my heart and hope to die."

"Well . . ." Starbuck lowered his voice. "I lose, but only when I want to. See what I mean?"

"You're not a cardsharp, are you?"

"No, ma'am!" Starbuck appeared wounded. "But when I set my mind to it, there's no man alive who's my equal at a poker table."

She suddenly looked quite enchanting. "Then I hope you beat them all! The sore losers most especially!"

"You know," Starbuck gently squeezed her hand. "I think I'm going to like this town."

She laughed softly. "I think you will, too."

Something in her voice startled him. Though he couldn't quite define it, he knew it wasn't to be discounted. There was more to Alice Blaylock than met the eye, something worth exploring. But for now, he played it for laughs.

"You're not making any promises, are you?"

"No." She gave him a mysterious smile. "Not yet."

CHAPTER 6

A haze of smoke hung suspended in the lamplight. The men seated around the poker table were a democratic admixture of the mining camp. There were three miners, a couple of teamsters, and a whiskey drummer. And Jack Johnson.

The hour was late and the game was slowly winding down. Starbuck, seated where he could watch the room, was the heavy winner. He lost often enough to keep the other players gaffed, but it was clearly his night. His mood was jovial, almost ingenuous, and he was at some pains to humor the losers. He was also cheating.

On the third finger of his left hand Starbuck wore a simple ring. The stone was common onyx, set in a plain gold band. It was unnoteworthy, and to all appearances of no great value. On the underside of the band, however, it was somewhat more remarkable. A small, all but invisible, needle point protruded from the bottom of the band. Among professional gamblers it was known as a "nicker" or "needle ring."

The ring provided Starbuck several advantages over

the other players. While dealing, early on in the game, he had pricked the face of key cards in the deck. This prick raised an imperceptible bump on the top of the card. Useless a man's fingertips were unusually sensitive, the bumps were virtually undetectable. Earlier, Starbuck had sandpapered the pads of his fingers, and as a result, it was somewhat like reading Braille. Simply by shuffling, he was able to identify almost half the cards in the deck.

Whenever he dealt, the coded bumps allowed him to locate key cards. Then, by dealing seconds, he was able to give himself the necessary cards for a winning hand. Since he also "read" the cards dealt to other players, he had several options. To avoid suspicion, he dealt himself a winner every fourth or fifth time around. The rest of the time, he dropped out and dealt a winning hand to a player whose luck had gone sour. With skill, and the law of averages, he also won his share of the hands dealt by others. No one suspected anything out of the ordinary, nor did they begrudge him what seemed a remarkable hot streak. It was a nifty dodge, and he worked it artfully.

Starbuck's purpose was to effect the next step in his courtship of Wyatt Earp. By establishing himself as a cardsharp—utterly lacking in honesty—he hoped to win acceptance within Earp's circle of cronies. He had selected tonight, only two days after his dinner with Alice, for the most expedient of reasons. Virgil Earp had wandered into the Alhambra shortly after the supper hour. Doc Holliday, whose own game broke up earlier than usual, had joined Virgil at the bar. As the night progressed, they had slowly, ever so gradually, worked their way to the end of the counter. From there, they had an unobstructed view of the poker table.

Starbuck scarcely glanced at them throughout the evening. Yet he was aware of their keen scrutiny whenever it came his turn to deal. Solely for their benefit, he staged a demonstration of dexterity and adroit card manipulation. Some years ago, as part of his undercover repertoire, he had taken lessons from a master cardsharp turned saloonkeeper. His performance, then, was not that of a tinhorn gambler. It was faultless, very professional, and thoroughly convincing.

Several times he saw them exchange glances with Earp. From the faro table, Earp nodded in return, and it seemed certain there was something more afoot than simple curiosity. He got the strong impression that Virgil Earp and Doc Holliday were waiting for his game to end. He had no idea what they intended, but the signals being passed were somehow ominous. Wyatt Earp, quite clearly, had rigged a surprise of his own for tonight.

Around midnight the poker game ground to a halt. Starbuck was easily a thousand dollars ahead, but no one seemed to take it personally. He told a bawdy joke—while pocketing his winnings—and left them laughing. It was the final touch, one he knew wouldn't be missed by the men at the bar. A true grifter always left his marks in a congenial frame of mind. Which made them all the easier to pluck next time around.

Walking to the bar, he was acutely aware that a new game was about to commence. He had no inkling as to its rules, nor did he know where it would lead. But he sensed it would be played in dead earnest.

"Evening, gents," he said cheerily. "Buy you a drink?"

Holliday wore his perpetually constipated expression, sour and tight-lipped. Virge's greeting was civil but cool. He nodded toward the poker table.

"How'd you come out?"

"Broke the game!" Starbuck crowed. "Damnedest run of luck you ever seen."

Holliday loosed a harsh bark of laughter. Suddenly his face reddened and he was racked by a spasm of coughing. Only after he managed to knock back a whiskey did the coughing subside. He glanced around, wiping tears from his eyes with a handkerchief.

"Some folks get shot for that kind of luck."

By now, Starbuck knew that Holliday was afflicted with consumption. Devoid of fear, since he was already on speaking terms with death, the cadaverous gambler had the edge in any fight. Whether he meant to provoke a showdown now was a moot question. Starbuck couldn't believe they had learned his true identity; but neither could he risk dropping his masquerade. He chose his words carefully.

"Outhouse luck, Doc! Here today, gone tomorrow!"

Before Holliday could respond, Virge quickly broke into the conversation. "Wyatt tells me you worked Leadville."

"A time or two," Starbuck said, wondering if he'd misread Holliday. "Not many camps I haven't worked."

"I heard Leadville's gone plumb to the dogs."

"Don't you believe it! There's easy pickings for any man that knows his way around."

"That's funny." Virge's bushy eyebrows seemed to hood his eyes. "Somebody told me Jeff Winney had folded the Texas House and gone on back to New Orleans."

Starbuck suddenly recognized the game. He was being grilled, and none too subtly. The Earps had apparently decided on one more test, with a trap thrown in for good measure. He swiftly turned it to advantage.

"That somebody," he laughed, "don't know his ass from his elbow about Leadville. First off, Bailey Youngston owns the Texas House, not Jeff Winney. And he's from down around Galveston way, not New Orleans. Hell, that's why he named his joint the Texas House!"

"Beats all!" Virge said levelly. "Fellow don't know who to believe no more."

Starbuck wedged his cheroot in the corner of his mouth. "Tell you what, Virge. It'd be like stealing money, but I'll lay you twenty to one that Jeff Winney never even set foot in the Texas House."

"No, you're likely right." Virge hesitated, then gave him a sharp sidelong look. "Wyatt says you come south for your health?"

"One of them things," Starbuck shrugged. "Some jasper went on the prod and I had to stop his clock."

"What set him off?"

"Would you believe it?" Starbuck said with mock indignity. "The sonovabitch accused me of cheating at cards!"

Holliday snorted and turned his eyes heavenward.

Virge bit down hard on a smile, seemingly stumped
for another question. After a moment, he shoved away
from the bar, flicking a glance in the direction of the
faro table. Then he consulted his watch.

"Well, boys, time flies. I gotta be gettin' home."

"I'll walk along," Holliday added. "Got a late game
waiting at the Oriental."

"Yeah?" Starbuck grinned. "Maybe I'll sit in a
while. The way my luck's running tonight, I can't be
beat."

Holliday examined him with a kind of cold objec-
tivity. Then he grunted something under his breath and
walked away. Virge and Starbuck fell in behind, following him toward the door. All the way along the
bar, Starbuck felt a strange sensation centered between
his shoulder blades. He had little doubt that Earp was
zeroed on him like a watchful chickenhawk.

Outside, Virge waved and turned uptown. Holliday
turned in the opposite direction, striding off toward the
Oriental. Starbuck trailed alongside him, and they
walked several paces in silence. Then Holliday riveted
him with a sullen stare.

"None of your tricks. It might work with those bo-
hunk miners, but I won't tolerate it in my game."

"So you caught that?" Starbuck laughed. "Christ, I
must be slipping."

"No, Johnson," Holliday said cynically, "you're not
slipping. You just weren't good enough to start with.
A needle ring, for God's sake!"

Starbuck's reply was cut short by the hammering
roar of gunfire. There were four blasts in rapid suc-
cession, and he instantly catalogued it as two men with

double-barrel shotguns. All in a split-second, he and Holliday whirled, drawing pistols. The street was empty and still.

Then they spotted Virge. He lay in the gutter, where the boardwalk dropped off to the street. The dim glow of the corner streetlamp bathed him in a spectral light. He was flat on his back, spraddle-legged and unmoving.

Starbuck sprinted to the corner, cautiously checking the sidestreet. There was no one in sight, and as he turned back, Holliday dropped to one knee beside Virge. In the glow of the streetlamp, he saw that the shotguns had done a savage job. The buckshot had blown away part of Virge's coat, and what lay underneath looked like freshly butchered beef. His left arm dangled by a thread of bone flesh at the elbow.

"Get Wyatt!" Holliday thundered. "Get him quick!"

Starbuck took off running toward the Alhambra.

A stark silence permeated the house. Everyone in the parlor was immobile, their eyes fixed on the hallway door. Their mood was one of people drawn together in a deathwatch, forlorn and without hope.

The entire Earp family, all the brothers and their wives, had gathered at Virge's home. Following the shooting, Starbuck and Earp had improvised a stretcher and carried him across town. Holliday, meanwhile, had gone to fetch Tombstone's only surgeon, Dr. George Goodfellow. Now, dreading the worst, they waited for the surgeon to emerge from the bedroom. He had been operating on Virge for nearly an hour.

Starbuck stood with Alice near the front door. She gripped his hand tightly, her face pale and drawn. His presence obviously comforted her, and thus far no one had objected to him intruding on a family affair. His expression was properly solemn, but he shared none of their concern. Whether Virge lived or died was the farthest thing from his mind. He was, instead, fascinated by the tableau of the Earp family.

Until tonight he hadn't fully appreciated their numbers. Earp, his features stony and cold, dominated the group. Seated around the room were Jim, the eldest brother, and his wife. Nearby were Morg and Warren, both younger and considerably more robust in appearance. Virge's wife, whose expression was ghastly, was huddled in a corner with Mattie and the other wives. Doc Holliday, sipping from a flask, stared morosely at a spot on the wall. Their silence was palpable, and strangely unnatural.

To an outsider, their stoicism was difficult to credit. Starbuck noted that Virge's wife, despite her hollow-eyed gaze, hadn't yet shed a tear. The three brothers, like Earp, were stolid as oxen. No one spoke, and no one registered the emotion normally expected under such circumstances. It was as though any public display of sentiment had been prohibited. Whatever they felt, whatever hurt and suffering they shared, was bottled up deep inside. The effect was eerie, somehow scary. Not unlike an assemblage of brutes contemplating a bleached skull.

The spell was broken as Dr. Goodfellow appeared in the hallway door. His sleeves were rolled up and his shirtfront was speckled with blood. His expression was grim.

Earp spoke for the family. "How is he, doc?"

"Alive," Godfellow said calmly. "I got all the buckshot out of his side and back. So far as I can tell, his spine wasn't damaged."

"What else?" Earp insisted. "Let's hear it all."

Goodfellow pursed his lips. "Wyatt, I'm sorry to say it doesn't look good. I may have to amputate his arm, but he's too weak to survive major surgery. We'll just have to wait and hope his condition improves."

"Will he pull through?"

"I wouldn't hazard a guess. Quite frankly, it could go either way."

"Why now?" Earp's iron impassivity suddenly deserted him. He turned away, his eyes garnet with rage. "Goddamnit, why now?"

Virge's wife rose from the settee and crossed the parlor. Without a word, Dr. Goodfellow took her arm and escorted her down the hall. A moment later there was a faint click as the bedroom door closed.

Morg abruptly jumped to his feet. "I'll tell you why! We waited too long. We should've gone after them the minute charges was dropped against you and Doc."

"He's right!" Warren blurted out. "Brocius and them bastards figured we was runnin' scared. Otherwise they wouldn't've never done that to Virge!"

"I second the motion." Holliday saluted them with his flask. "Get them before they get us! I told Wyatt that very thing myself."

Starbuck looked from one to the other, spellbound.

He knew Morg had killed a man in the shootout at the OK Corral, and Warren was reportedly no slouch with a gun as well. Unbidden, a thought popped into his head. He realized he was listening to a brotherhood of murderers. Not just Earp and Holliday, but the entire family. All of them were cold-blooded killers.

"Take the fight to them!" Morg said vindictively. "If we don't, they're gonna pick us off one by one just as sure as hell."

Warren nodded vigorously. "The same way they did Virge!"

"Better listen, Wyatt," Holliday affirmed. "You keep trying to polish your image, and we're all liable to go up the flume."

"That'll do!" Earp said sternly. "We'll move when I say so, and not before."

"You and your damn politics!" Morg exploded. "It's not worth it, Wyatt! Not anymore."

A strained stillness settled over the room. Earp's jaw muscles knotted and a vein pulsed in his forehead. His brothers seemed to shrink back under his scowl, and he stared at them for several moments. Then, remembering himself, his gaze shuttled to Starbuck. His look once more became stolid, impenetrable.

"You boys," he admonished his brothers, "forgot we have company. Let's leave it till another time."

Starbuck took the hint. "Listen, I didn't mean to butt in on family business. I'll get on back to the hotel and catch some shut-eye."

"I'm obliged to you," Earp said quietly. "Virge and me owe you one."

"Forget it," Starbuck replied, opening the door. "I

was glad to lend a hand. Let me know how Virge gets along."

Alice walked him outside. She looked stunned. Her eyes were dulled and her features were completely drained of color. He took her hands, searching her face in the pale starlight.

"What's wrong?"

"I'm afraid," she told him. "The killing has started again, and it won't end here."

"Don't worry," Starbuck gently advised. "Wyatt and his brothers can take care of themselves."

"It's not them!" She squeezed his hands fiercely. "I'm worried about you."

"Here now," Starbuck chuckled. "You've got no call to worry about me. I'm an old hand at looking after number one."

"Get out now!" she said vehemently. "Don't let Wyatt draw you into his fight."

"All things considered, he's treated me pretty square."

"Wyatt doesn't have friends! He uses people and"— her voice became a desperate whisper—"they end up dead."

Starbuck lifted her chin, smiled. "You can ease your mind on that score. I aim to live a long time."

The door opened and Earp stepped onto the porch. As he moved down the stairs, Alice brushed past him and hurried inside the house. He glanced back at her, then halted in front of Starbuck.

"She upset?"

"Some," Starbuck admitted. "It's been a bad night."

"Bad as they come," Earp agreed. "I'm a little

touchy myself. Otherwise I wouldn't have cut you off
so quick a minute ago."

"Don't give it another thought. No offense taken."

"Good." Earp paused, studying the ground. "Doc
tells me you've got troubles of your own."

"Leadville?" Starbuck wagged his head. "No, that's
likely water under the bridge by now."

"Wish ours were," Earp said bitterly. "Way things
look, there's rough times ahead."

"Well, listen here now! You need any help, all
you've got to do is holler. I mean it!"

"I appreciate the offer, Jack. And I'm not one to
forget a favor."

"What the hell!" Starbuck flipped a palm back and
forth. "Us gamblin' men have got to stick together."

Earp shook his hand warmly and they parted. Walking toward town, Starbuck had to restrain himself from
laughing out loud. Tonight had worked out even better
than he'd planned. Especially where Earp was concerned.

The sorry bastard had taken the bait, hook and all!

CHAPTER 7

For New Year's Eve, the diningroom in the hotel had been-cleared of furniture. Gaudy bunting and little Japanese lanterns festooned the ceiling, and the floor had been waxed to a mirror polish. The Volunteer Firemen's band thumped sedately over the strains of an upright piano.

Alice looked ravishing tonight. Her hair, dark as a raven's wing, was arranged in an upswept style that accentuated her oval features. Her eyes sparkled and her mouth seemed poised for laughter. She was animated and vivacious, and for one night she was clearly determined to set aside worldly troubles. She smelled sweet and alluring, and she clung joyously to Starbuck.

Holding her at arm's length, Starbuck swung her gracefully across the dance floor. For a large man, he was surprisingly light on his feet. His step was better suited to the stomping beat of a dancehall, but he managed the waltz without once stepping on her toes. It was their first dance of the evening, and already he knew he'd gauged her mood correctly. Her eyes never left his face, and her dreamy expression spoke louder than words. She was his for the asking, and he sensed she would deny him nothing. Tonight was the night all her secrets would be revealed.

When the dance ended, they walked toward a refreshment table near the front of the room. The crowd was steadily increasing, and a large throng was congregated around the punchbowl. Though other hotels were holding dances, the Occidental's gala was considered the only affair suitable for decent people. Tombstone's uppercrust, merchants and bankers and mine owners, formed a snobbish, tightly knit society all their own. So far, Starbuck and Alice had been treated with polite diffidence. A gambler and his lady weren't particularly welcome, but no one seemed inclined to make an issue of it. The general consensus was apparently one of benign tolerance.

Then, quite suddenly, the atmosphere changed. A buzz of conversation swept over the room, and Starbuck noticed that people were staring toward the entrance. Turning, he saw Morg and Warren Earp, accompanied by their wives, standing in the wide doorway leading to the lobby. As the foursome advanced into the room, the murmur from the crowd took on an ugly note. Couples near the doorway quickly moved to the opposite side of the dance floor. The Earps and their women were left in an uncomfortable vacuum.

Starbuck took Alice's hand and led her across the floor. He totally ignored the stares of onlookers and their muttered comments. With a wide grin, he greeted the Earps, shaking hands forcefully. Their wives looked painfully embarrassed, and he had no doubt the brothers had forced them to attend the dance. As usual, the women wore dresses that appeared to have been purchased at a rummage sale. The men, by comparison, were dandified fashion plates.

"Glad you folks made it," Starbuck said warmly. "I haven't seen a familiar face since we got here."

"You likely won't, either." Morg shook his head in disgust. "Our kind isn't exactly welcome at this shindig."

"Say listen, don't let this bunch of swells put your nose out of joint. It's New Year's Eve!"

"They don't seem to bother you none."

"Nosiree!" Starbuck jerked a thumb toward the crowd. "Anybody looks cross-eyed at me and I'll tell'em to stuff it where the sun don't shine."

"Jack!" Alice giggled. "They'll hear you."

"So what?" Starbuck said loudly. "Maybe an earful would do them good."

Morg burst out laughing. "You're a regular rooster, aren't you?"

"Live and let live, that's my motto."

Starbuck was mentally calculating how the moment could be turned to advantage. Thus far, he'd had no opportunity to speak with the two youngest Earp brothers. He judged Morg to be in his mid-twenties, and Warren a year or so behind. From their one meeting, he had sized them up as youthful hotheads, and therefore vulnerable. A man whose temper ruled his tongue often talked too much for his own good. What, if anything, they might reveal was sheer speculation. But it was very definitely worth a try.

"How's Virge?" Starbuck went on, suddenly sober. "Any improvement?"

"Not a whole lot," Morg said in an aggrieved tone. "He'll pull through, but it's touch and go with his arm."

"That sawbones still want to amputate?"

"Hard to say. This afternoon he told Wyatt there's no sign of gangrene. But he wouldn't commit himself one way or the other."

"Wyatt over at the Alhambra tonight?"

"No," Morg remarked. "Him and Doc are at Virge's. We're taking turns watching the house."

"You really think Brocius would try it again?"

"That crazy jaybird's liable to try anything."

Starbuck appeared thoughtful. "What's Brocius like, anyway? Crazy crazy or crazy like a fox?"

"What makes you ask?"

"Well, for one thing, he don't seem to take too many chances. He steered clear of that shootout you had with his boys, and now he ambushes Virge. Offhand, I'd say he's a pretty slick article."

"Slick, hell!" Warren struck into the conversation with an oath. "He's a dirty yellow bushwhacker! Why d'you think he got Virge in the back that way?"

"I was wondering about that," Starbuck said lazily. "What made him pick Virge? Why not Wyatt or Doc?"

"Who knows?" Warren snapped. "More'n likely he took whoever come along first."

"Queer, though, isn't it?"

"I don't follow you."

"Tell you the truth, I don't rightly follow myself. I

guess I was trying to puzzle out what's behind it."

"What's behind what?"

"Why he wants blood so bad. A man's got to hate awful strong to shoot somebody after all that time."

"Seems simple enough to me," Morg explained. "Virge was marshal the day we killed three of his men."

"But it's not just Virge," Starbuck insisted. "You said the other night he was after the whole family."

Morg's mouth hardened. "Are you sayin' he's not?"

"No, nothing like that! I'm just asking why—why he wants all of you?"

"Same reason," Morg said flatly. "We all had a hand in his men gettin' killed."

"Yeah, maybe." Starbuck looked doubtful. "But if he just wanted revenge, why did he wait so long? One dark night's as good as another."

"Tell you what." Morg's eyes suddenly became guarded. "Why don't you ask Brocius? If he's got other reasons, then he's keepin' them to himself. All I know is what I told you."

Starbuck decided to let it drop. The exchange had failed to provoke anything of value, and Morg was clearly growing suspicious. He spread his hands in an empty gesture.

"Hell, maybe he's just plain crazy after all. There's an old saying that some men will commit suicide in order to commit murder. Way it looks, he fits the ticket all the way round."

The band segued into another waltz and he held out his hand to Alice. She stepped into his arms and they joined the crowd on the dance floor. Waving to the

Earps, he grinned broadly and left them once more in their vacuum. Several minutes later he saw them turn and walk out through the lobby. He had gained nothing from the discussion, but he was in no way discouraged. The night, and Alice, still held great promise.

At midnight Tombstone's gentry lost some of their highfalutin ways. The band struck up "Auld Lang Syne," and sedate revelers were instantly transformed into riotous merrymakers. A lusty roar shook the rafters, and the prohibition not to covet thy neighbor's wife was momentarily suspended. The crowd swirled together in a mass kissing bee.

Starbuck took Alice's face in his hands and brushed her lips with a soft kiss. She regarded him a moment with an odd steadfast look. Then her arms circled his neck and she pulled his mouth to hers in a sensuous invitation. He responded, enfolding her tightly within his arms. When they parted, he gave her a suggestive smile.

"Too bad we never get any privacy."

Her voice was husky. "There's really no way . . . to be alone."

"I know a place."

"You do?"

"Upstairs." Starbuck rolled his eyes upward. "There's lots of privacy in my room."

"I—" She stopped, unable to meet his gaze. "I'm afraid, Jack. The desk clerk would see us and then . . . everyone would know."

"Not through the lobby." Starbuck nuzzled her ear,

lowering his voice. "The backstairs, behind the hotel. Nobody would see us there, especially now."

"Oh?" she said in an indrawn breath. "Are you sure?"

"Positive," Starbuck assured her. "Take a look around. They're all too busy making fools of themselves."

She darted a glance at the boisterous crowd. Then she moved closer, like a seductive butterfly. A ghost of a smile touched her lips, and she gave him a bright nod.

"I do want to be alone with you, Jack."

Their departure went unnoticed. Starbuck took her hand and they walked out through the lobby. Behind them, the revelers were still shouting and kissing and tooting paper horns. The desk clerk, stifling a bored yawn, scarcely looked at them.

Outside the hotel, Starbuck checked both ways along the street. Several drunks were gathered near a corner saloon, but the boardwalks were otherwise deserted. Walking to the side of the building, he wheeled sharply left and they vanished into the alley. Several seconds later he led her up the backstairs and through a second-floor doorway. The hall was empty and he quickly fished the room key out of his pocket. Ushering her inside, he locked the door and tossed his hat in the direction of the bureau. Then he turned and gathered her into his arms.

Whatever he expected, he was not prepared for the urgency of her embrace. Her lips were soft and moist, and her mouth parted in a hunger born of loneliness and need. She kissed him long and passionately, her

body pressed fiercely against his own. He felt her
breasts pushing into him and her hips moving against
his loins. She moaned as he caressed her back and
fondled the rounded curves of her bottom. A convul-
sion gripped her and her nails pierced his coat like
talons.

He lifted her in his arms and carried her toward the
bed.

A long while later she lay with her head nestled deep
in the hollow of his shoulder. Her hair, unbound and
falling loose, fanned darkly across the pillow. She
slept like a naked child clutching something warm and
familiar in the dark.

Starbuck was awake and thoughtful. He believed he
possessed a special sixth sense. A kind of visceral instinct that cut through the tangled skein of emotion
and reasoned logic. He had learned to accept it and
trust it, something far more reliable than mere hunch.
When it came over him, there was no blurred uncer-
tainty, no troubling doubt. Too many times that instinct alone had saved his life. He survived because
he'd always obeyed his gut, not his head.

Tonight that sense of conviction had never been
stronger. But with it came something new and unsettling. He felt a stab of conscience.

The girl beside him was no virgin, but neither was
she a whore. Somewhere in the midst of their love-
making that inner certainty had washed over him. She
was unlike the other Earp women, an innocent among
rogues. There was nothing to substantiate the feeling,
no word or act, no deductive explanation. He simply

knew she was not, either in mind or spirit, a part of the Earp family. She was an outsider, alien to all with the possible exception of her sister. His instinct told him it was true.

The realization made him uncomfortable with himself. He had deceived her, strung her along, and purposely kindled her affection. Now, under false pretenses, he had brought her to his bed and stoked that affection even higher. His conscience, which he normally kept whipped into submission, had suddenly rebelled. He wasn't at all sure that the end still justified the means.

Seldom introspective, he was a man with few illusions left intact. He saw life and people as they were, through a prism of cold reality. The dead men littering his backtrail had taught him that a cynic was rarely disappointed. Yet the girl lying peacefully in his arms deserved a better shake. Thus far he'd used her, and if his investigation was to succeed, he must continue to use her. While she might be an outsider to the Earps, she was his only inside source of information. To level with her could very well jeopardize that source. Expediency dictated that he play on her affections, and guile her into revealing whatever she knew. The idea was no longer abstract, some impersonal, though essential, part of the job. He would do it, but the thought left him troubled inside. He saw a part of himself he didn't much like.

"Penny for your thoughts."

Her voice broke into his reverie. He glanced down and found her watching him with a warm smile. Quickly, all regret shunted aside, he got on with the task. He grinned, gently stroking her hair.

"Why spoil the evening?"

"Good Lord!" She squirmed around, lifting herself on one elbow. "Now you have to tell me."

"Well—" Starbuck paused for effect, then shrugged. "I was just thinking you're not too wild about your brother-in-law."

"Wyatt?"

"Yeah, him most especially. But I get the idea you don't care much for any of that crowd."

She stared at him in silence, her dark eyes filled with some buried emotion. "What makes you say that?"

"Tricks of the trade. A gambler gets to be a pretty good judge of people."

"I suppose it's no secret," she said, not without bitterness. "For Mattie's sake, Wyatt and I tolerate each other."

Starbuck could see anger and a trace of fear in her eyes. "Why is it I get the feeling you're afraid of him?"

Her words were almost inaudible, so quiet he had to strain to hear. "Because I am."

"Afraid?"

"Scared to death."

"Why?" Starbuck inquired evenly. "Wyatt seems like a pleasant enough sort."

"You don't know him."

"I know he's got a reputation with a gun. But the way I hear it, he had cause."

"Did he?"

"Wait a minute." Starbuck looked confused. "Are

we talking about the same thing? I understood him and Doc were cleared of that shooting scrape."

"They were," she murmured uneasily. "Only there was more to it than that."

The admission startled Starbuck. He sensed she was hinting at the death of Marsh Williams, the Wells, Fargo agent. He warned himself to proceed with caution.

"You mean there was something that didn't come out in court?"

"Not something." She tossed her head. "Everything!"

"Damnation!" Starbuck chuckled lightly. "Don't tell me he gunned down somebody else!"

"Jack—" She hesitated, exploring his face. "I'm acting silly, and talking very foolish. Please forget I said anything, will you? Promise me, Jack . . . please?"

"Count it done," Starbuck nodded. "But don't wait 'til things get out of hand. If you ever need help, all you have to do is yell."

"Oh, Jack." She kissed him tenderly. "You don't know how much that means to me."

Starbuck thought he knew very well. She was quite obviously terrified of Wyatt Earp. Yet, on the other hand, her hatred for him was barely contained. At the right time, under the proper circumstances, both her terror and her hatred could be exploited to the fullest. Until then, he could afford to be patient. And sympathetic.

"One thing's for sure," Starbuck said absently. "Wyatt must have some powerful business connections."

"Business connections?"

"Why, sure. Otherwise he would've been railroaded out of town long before now."

She stared gravely into his eyes. "I know nothing about his business. And I don't want to know."

Starbuck knew he had touched another nerve. But that too could await the right moment. He cupped her chin in his hand.

"All I meant was, you don't have to worry about him or his connections. You just whistle and I'll come running."

She shifted in his arms, and he pulled her into a tight embrace. His hand covered one of her jutting breasts and the nipple swelled instantly. Then her hand touched his manhood, erect and throbbing, and she grasped it eagerly. She was ready for him, damp and yielding, and she uttered a low moan as he penetrated quickly, slipped deep within her.

He gave her salvation, and hope.

CHAPTER 8

A week later Starbuck's patience began wearing thin. His nerves were gritty and restless, and he had a sense of marking time. His investigation had gone nowhere.

The evening was crisp and chill. He paused on the hotel veranda, lighting a cheroot. For a moment, he debated calling on Alice. Her company would be far more enjoyable than spending another night watching Earp and Holliday. Still, however tedious, he wasn't one to shirk responsibility. There was a job to be done, and Alice could contribute little or nothing at this point. He walked toward the Alhambra.

On balance, Starbuck had to admit he was stymied. After the attempt on Virge's life, he had expected action of some sort. He wasn't certain what form that action would take; but he'd felt reasonably confident it would lead to a break in the case. The last thing he'd expected was what Wyatt Earp had actually done. Nothing.

To whatever purpose, Earp was playing a waiting game. Shortly after New Year's, he and Holliday had reverted to their normal routine. Every night found

them at the Alhambra, business as usual. They were
more cautious now, particularly on the streets after
dark. But there was no mention of Curly Bill Brocius,
and no hint that retaliation of any nature was in the
works. To all appearances, it was as though the assassination attempt had never occurred.

Starbuck was at a loss. He needed something con-
crete to make a case, some tangible evidence. Yet that
was heavily dependent on worming his way into
Earp's confidence. So far, the ploy hadn't worked.
Earp trusted him, but Earp didn't need him. And there
was the crux of the matter. To become a member of
the clique, it was necessary that Earp need his services,
and his gun. Only then would Earp and the other members of the family speak freely around him. Equally
apparent, only then would he have access to evidence
linking them to robbery and murder. The fly in the
butter was all too obvious. His gun simply wasn't
needed.

On one side, Earp seemed content to sit on his
thumb. On the other, Brocius and his gang had attempted no further treachery. The vendetta appeared
to have degenerated into a stalemate, with neither side
disposed to make the next move. It was a sorry mess,
and getting sorrier all the time.

Entering the Alhambra, Starbuck found Holliday
nursing a drink at the bar. While the evening was still
early, Earp already had several players ganged around
the faro layout. Starbuck waved, receiving Earp's nod
in return, and moved toward the end of the counter.
Halting beside Holliday, he signaled the barkeep.

"No game tonight, Doc?"

Holliday frowned. "Some of the regulars ought to drift in later."

"Maybe I'll sit in."

"We'll likely have a full table."

"Not afraid of the competition, are you, Doc?"

"There's your game." Holliday indicated a group of miners, seated at one of the poker tables. "Those boys are just about your speed."

The barkeep poured Starbuck a drink, and he took a long sip. Then he smacked his lips, grinning. "You know what your trouble is, Doc?"

"I'm fresh out of guesses."

"You're worried a smooth article like me might slip one past you."

"That'll be the day," Holliday said glumly. "I could spot you dealin' seconds with my eyes closed."

"Yeah, and I can deal'em with *my* eyes closed, too!"

"Johnson, you've got more brass than a barrel of monkeys. I'll give you that much."

Starbuck was aware that Holliday hadn't fully accepted him. There was still a tinge of skepticism in the gambler's attitude. And perhaps an element of resentment as well. Holliday was jealous of anyone who got close to Earp. His spite took the form of sarcasm and belittling remarks, and the personal rancor was openly apparent. His soliloquy on Bat Masterson was a gem of character assassination.

Pondering on it, Starbuck had concluded that Holliday had only one friend in the entire world. The greater curiosity was that he had fooled himself into believing the loyalty went both ways. In truth, Earp

used him and would readily discard him if ever he
became a liability. The paradox was that a cynic like
Holliday deceived no one but himself. Had he asked,
anyone in Tombstone could have told him he was expendable.

Holliday suddenly stiffened. Following the direction of his gaze, Starbuck saw Sheriff John Behan
walking toward them. Though he knew the lawman on
sight, he'd never had occasion to exchange so much
as a greeting. His instinct told him that was about to
change.

Behan stopped a couple of paces away. He was a
stocky bulldog of a man, with a square tough face and
humorless eyes. Starbuck guessed he was the type who
wouldn't smile easily, if at all.

"Holliday, I'd like a word with you."

"What's on your mind, Sheriff?"

"The Benson stage."

Holliday faced him directly. "What about it?"

"A couple of hours ago," Behan said in a flinty
voice, "four men robbed the stage outside Contention."

"So?"

"So I'm askin' where you were about sundown."

"Standin' right here!" Holliday bristled with indig-
nation. "Not that it's any of your business."

"Anytime a stage gets robbed, I make it my business. Can you prove you were here?"

"I don't have to prove it."

"Yeah, you do. Unless you'd rather take a walk
down to the cooler."

"Back off!" Holliday said sharply. "You've got nothing on me."

"The driver," Behan informed him, "says one of the robbers fitted your description. That'll do for openers."

Holliday fixed him with a baleful look. "I haven't set foot out of here, not once."

"He's giving it to you straight, Sheriff."

Earp halted at the lawman's elbow. Behan moved back as though he'd been stung by a wasp. His mouth set in a hard grimace.

"I don't recall askin' you, Earp."

"I'm tellin' you," Earp said tightly, "whether you ask or not. Doc's been here all evening."

"You alibied him the last time I arrested him."

"And it held up in court. You ought to know by now, Doc don't have to rob stages for a living."

"How about you?"

"Careful, Behan." There was a hard edge to Earp's tone. "Don't push your luck."

"Are you threatening an officer of the law?"

"I'm telling you not to come in here and rawhide honest citizens. If it's stage robbers you're after, why don't you take a crack at Brocius and his gang?"

Behan eyed him keenly. "You'd like that, wouldn't you?"

"Damn right!" Earp said shortly. "After the way they ambushed Virge, I don't reckon they'd be above robbin' a stage."

"Suppose we stick with you and Holliday."

"Are you accusin' me, too?"

"I'm not accusing anybody. I'm askin' you to explain your whereabouts, and I mean to have an answer."

"You've already had your answer."

"That's not good enough," Behan countered. "You and Holliday would alibi one another till hell freezes over."

"Try me, then." Starbuck's voice was firm. "I'll vouch for both of them."

Behan looked him over like a mule he was considering buying, "Johnson, isn't it?"

"Jack Johnson," Starbuck acknowledged. "I've been here since suppertime, and it's like Doc says. They haven't set foot out of the place."

"You'd swear to that, would you?"

"On a stack of bibles ten feet tall."

"You might just have to do that, Johnson."

Behan spun on his heel and stalked out. When the door closed, everyone realized the room had gone still as a church. The crowd suddenly stopped gawking and the hubbub of conversation rose to a deafening pitch. Earp shook his head in disgust, exchanging a veiled glance with Holliday. Then his gaze shifted to Starbuck.

"Wasn't no need to lie, Jack. I appreciate the gesture, but anybody could tell him you'd just walked in here."

"Hell's bells!" Starbuck laughed. "A little white lie never hurt nobody. Specially a lawdog!"

"Well, all the same, we're obliged. Aren't we, Doc?"

"Johnson," Holliday clapped him on the shoulder. "How'd you like to take a chair in my game tonight?"

"Doc, I think we'd make a puredee fortune to-gether."

"None of your tricks! You hear me? Keep it straight!"

Starbuck grinned. "You've got yourself a deal, Doc. Straight as an arrow, that's me!"

Late that night Starbuck parted company with Earp and Holliday. He mounted the stairs of the hotel ve-randa, watching a moment as they continued up the street. Then he moved inside, quietly closing the door behind him. The night clerk, dozing fitfully on one of the couches, continued snoring. He catfooted across the lobby.

Upstairs, he walked directly to the rear door. On the landing outside, he paused and surveyed the dark-ened alley. Then, satisfied no one was around, he went down the backstairs. He turned left and hurried to the corner. There, he checked in both directions before darting across the street. With utmost caution, he worked his way from alley to alley, hugging the shad-ows whenever possible. His general direction was north, toward Safford Street.

As he skulked through town, Starbuck's thoughts were confused, speculative. There was something strange about tonight's stage robbery. He knew Earp and Holliday weren't involved, but the robbery seemed somehow part of a broader pattern. Over the past two weeks he had forged a tenuous link between Earp and the Brocius gang. Though the proof was still to come, the obstacles had not seemed to him insur-mountable. Yet tonight had introduced an element that left him baffled. The robbery had triggered the realization that a piece was missing. The sum of the known parts suddenly no longer added up to a whole. The jigsaw puzzle was incomplete.

Starbuck now considered the situation intolerable. Something was about to happen—or had already happened—and he sensed it would have a profound effect on the case. Yet he hadn't the vaguest notion of what it was, or who had done it. Nor was there any defensive measure he could take to counteract its effect. Not only was he fighting in the dark, he was grappling with an unknown, and that left him only one recourse. He had to take the offensive—and fast.

A half hour later he paused in the alleyway behind Harry Woods' home. He waited several minutes, wondering if Woods kept a yard dog, then decided there was no way to avoid the risk. He walked quickly to the back door, flattening himself in the shadows. He rapped lightly with his knuckles, listening a moment. Then he rapped harder.

The wait seemed interminable. At last, the glow of a lamp lighted the house. Through the window, he saw Woods appear in a hallway, dressed in a nightshirt. The editor entered the kitchen and hurried to the back door.

"Who is it?"

"A friend," Starbuck said in a muffled voice. "Douse the light."

The lamp went out and Woods slipped the door latch. "Come in, Luke."

"Sorry to bother you so late at night."

"It's quite all right."

Starbuck stepped into the kitchen. Woods locked the door, then moved around the room pulling windowshades. A match flared and he relit the lamp. His eyes were gummed with sleep and he peered at Starbuck like a weary gnome.

"What's wrong, Luke?"

"We've got trouble," Starbuck told him. "I need your help."

"Here, sit down." Woods pulled out a chair at the kitchen table. "What's Earp done now?"

"Harry, I wish to hell I knew."

Starbuck straddled a chair and began talking. He briefed Woods on the stage robbery and Sheriff Behan's visit to the Alhambra. Then, omitting the spicier details, he related the extent of his progress with Alice Blaylock. Finally, he gave a rundown on his dealings with Earp and Holliday, and the Earp brothers. He kept it brief, but covered all the salient points.

"That's about it," he concluded. "Or leastways as much as means anything."

Woods looked impressed. "I would say you've made excellent progress. What seems to be the problem?"

"Not *the* problem," Starbuck commenced in a sandy voice. "A whole batch of problems! Earp acts like he's waiting on an egg to hatch. I don't see any sign of him taking the trail against Brocius. And unless he does, then there's no reason for him to ask my help." He paused, slowly shook his head. "On top of all that, I've got a gut-sure hunch there's something I don't know. Something damned important."

"Oddly enough," Woods observed, "I was seriously

debating whether or not to contact you. It's just possible Earp has already hatched his egg."

"How's that?"

"Let me start at the beginning," Woods replied. "You may recall you asked me to check into Earp's business interests. With no one the wiser, I was able to gain access to both the town and county tax records. It turns out that Mr. Earp is a man of some means."

Starbuck suddenly came alert. "He owns property?"

"Several properties," Woods corrected. "Some in his own name and some in the names of various family members. Altogether, the Earp family owns eleven town lots outright. More importantly, Earp has a fifty-fifty interest in four rather substantial mining properties."

"Fifty-fifty?" Starbuck furrowed his brow. "Who owns the other half?"

"Some of the most prominent businessmen in Tombstone. Their names wouldn't mean anything to you, but they went to great pains to keep their dealings with Earp an absolute secret. Much of it was done through lawyers and paper corporations."

"Sounds like you've done a bit of detective work yourself."

"Indeed, I have," Woods admitted. "It's taken me the better part of two weeks, and led me through a maze of legal hocus-pocus. But I think it yielded some rather impressive dividends."

"Damn right!" Starbuck confirmed. "Our faro dealer turns out to be something more than he appears."

"He's a sly and devious man. I think it's fair to say

he was creating powerful alliances that would have eventually led to political control of Cochise County. After that, there would have been no stopping him."

"Lift a rock and find a scorpion." Starbuck was silent a moment, thoughtful. "You said something about him already having hatched his egg. Were you referring to this political alliance?"

"Not entirely," Woods remarked. "I'm not sure what it means, but this afternoon I happened across a curious piece of information. Within the last two weeks or so, Earp has sold his interest in three of the mining properties. He's also unloaded eight of the town lots."

"Goddamn!" Starbuck slammed his fist down on the table. "That's it!"

Woods was startled. "That's what?"

"The missing piece!" Starbuck said quickly. "He's getting ready to run."

"I fail to see the connection."

"Virge was shot on December 28. That's ten days ago, and Earp started selling off his properties right after it happened. He's just waiting around till Virge is well enough to travel. Then he's going to make dust for parts unknown."

"Hmmm?" Woods considered a moment. "You know something, Luke? It makes sense. Very good sense!"

"Maybe for Earp," Starbuck conceded. "But I don't like it one damn bit. Matter of fact, we'll have to move quicker than I thought."

"Quicker?"

"Harry, I want you to write an article about Behan

bracing Earp and Holliday. Play it up big! Tell the whole world how Earp stood right up in the Alhambra and laid the robbery off on Brocius. Tell them how he accused Brocius of ambushing Virge. Put it in big black headlines that he called Brocius a coward and a dirty yellow bushwhacker. Smear it all over the front page. No holds barred!"

Woods appeared puzzled. "To what purpose? What do you hope to accomplish?"

"I mean to push somebody into making a mistake."

"Earp?"

"Or Brocius," Starbuck nodded. "I want one of them to start shooting, and I don't much care which side kicks it off."

"Then Earp enlists your help and you become a member of the club . . . correct?"

Starbuck smiled. "That's the general idea."

"You're pretty devious yourself, Luke."

"I try," Starbuck said, grinning. "One other thing. When you get a minute, check out the dates Earp bought each of those properties."

"May I ask why?"

"So we can compare the purchase dates with a list of dates that stages were robbed. I'm betting we'll get a pretty close match."

Woods blinked. "Not even Earp would be that— arrogant."

"Harry, I've learned one thing about crooks and desperadoes. I've never yet seen it fail."

"What's that?"

"All of them," Starbuck laughed, "confuse balls with brains."

CHAPTER 9

The Clanton ranch lay in the foothills of the Whetstone Mountains. Across the vast emptiness there was a sense of desolation. The land sloped sharply downward as it stretched toward the San Pedro River, broken occasionally by buttes and treacherous arroyos.

Some miles west of Tombstone, there was no road as such leading to the ranch. Instead, a rutted trail bordered the river, eventually ending at a remote settlement called Charleston. On the afternoon of January 10 a rider appeared southward along the trail. His horse was lathered and spent, but he held it to a gallop as he rode toward the ranch headquarters. A ramshackle collection of buildings, the compound consisted of a main house, a cook shack and bunkhouse, and a log corral. No working ranch, it was a waystation for Mexican cattle rustled by the Brocius gang.

The rider slid his horse to a dust-smothered halt before the house. Vaulting from the saddle, he left the horse wheezing and near collapse. Hurrying forward, he jerked a soiled newspaper from his coat pocket and burst through the door. Inside, he slammed to a stop and waved the newspaper aloft.

"You ain't gonna believe what I got here!"

The men sprawled around the room were a rough lot. Their clothes were rank, and with the exception of one man, none of them had taken a bath since the last time it rained. The smell of unwashed bodies, stale food, and rotgut whiskey left the room permeated with a rainbow of odors. For several moments, no one spoke. They stared at the man holding the newspaper with looks of bored disinterest. Finally, he advanced toward a large man slouched down in a rickety chair. He shook the newspaper as though swatting flies.

"You made the front page, Bill! Wyatt Earp says you're—"

Bill Brocius snatched the paper out of his hand. A huge man, wide and tall, Brocius had thick curly hair and full mustaches. He snapped the paper open and began reading. His lips moved as he labored with the words, and his face slowly colored to the hairline. A leaden silence ensued while he scanned the article. Then he suddenly balled the newspaper into a wad and hurled it across the room.

"That sonovabitch!" he snarled. "Gawddamn if he couldn't lie his way out of a locked safe!"

Pete Spence, who had brought the newspaper, wisely took a chair. Frank Stilwell glanced at Johnny Ringo, who was slumped in a battered, cane-bottomed rocker. On a dilapidated sofa, Ike and Finn Clanton, owners of the ranch, exchanged a quick look. At last, Ike leaned forward and retrieved the newspaper. Unwadding it, he moved back beside his brother, and skimmed through the article. His mouth popped open in astonishment.

"Talk about the pot callin' the kettle black! The dirty scutter out and out accuses us of robbin' the Benson stage."

"That ain't no lie," Stilwell chuckled. "Unless I was dreamin', we did."

"Mebbe so," Finn Clanton allowed. "But he's still got no call to be sayin' it out loud."

"Why not?"

"Because he ain't so clean himself. That's why!"

"You'd play hell provin' it, and don't nobody know it better than him."

"Oh yeah?" Ike Clanton chimed in. "How about all them times Holliday give us the lowdown on stage shipments?"

"That was Holliday, not Earp."

"Same difference!" Finn retorted. "Earp don't itch without Holliday scratchin' his ass."

"I'm not sayin' otherwise. I just said we ain't got no proof of that."

"Johnny does!" Finn said positively. "Earp slipped up once't, and was standin' right there when Holliday gave Johnny the dope. Ain't that right, Johnny?"

Ringo lolled back in his rocker, one leg hooked over the chair arm. "You've got a big mouth, Finn."

"Awww—" Finn Clanton's wise-ass smile faded under his cold stare. "C'mon, Johnny! I didn't mean no harm."

"Then button your lip and leave my name out of it."

Ringo was swarthy man, with muddy eyes and sleek, glistening hair. He was clean-shaven, neatly dressed, and smelled like a lily compared to the others. Among all the gang members, he was the one authentic *pistolero*. Some years ago, when his brother was murdered in Texas, he had tracked down the four killers and dispatched them in *mano a mano* gunfights. When angered, his face became stern as a deacon's and his eyes turned to chilled stone. The other men saw that look now, and prudently left him to himself.

Ike Clanton, who was again perusing the newspaper article, suddenly erupted. "Dirty rotten sheep-humper! You boys wanna hear what Mr. Godalmighty Earp thinks of us?"

"Sure thing!" Stilwell cackled. "Couldn't be no worse'n what we think of him."

"He says"—Ike squinted hard at the paper—"and this here's his own words, 'Bill Brocius is a yellow-livered coward. He and his gang of penny-ante badmen drygulched my bother with never a chance. They are nothing but bushwhackers and backshooters, the lowest form of vermin known to man.' That's what he called us! Them exact words!"

Everyone turned to look at Brocius. He glowered back at them, outrage stamped across his face. He shook a finger at Ike.

"Keep readin' and you'll find out he said all that standin' at the bar in the Alhambra. Made himself a regular gawddamn speech! Told it to the world and anybody that'd listen."

"Bastard!" Finn muttered. "He's sure got a lot of room to talk, don't he?"

Stilwell looked confused. "What d'you mean?"

"What he means," Brocius rumbled, "is that Earp and his brothers make us look like pikers. They're nothin' but common murderers, and pretty damn open about it! Ain't that right, Ike?"

Ike Clanton flushed beet red. Any mention of the OK Corral shootout brought the bright light of shame to his eyes. On that October day, less than three months past, he had shown the white feather. As the Earps and Holliday approached the livery stable, he had darted forward, screaming hysterically that he was unarmed. Then, as the shooting commenced, he had taken refuge in a nearby photographer's studio. From there, he watched the final execution of his own brother, Billy Clanton, and the two McLowery brothers. He was the lone survivor, and it was simple cowardice that had saved his life. The memory of that day had dimmed none at all. He still burned with guilt, and the other gang members held him in studied contempt.

"I'll tell you one thing," he said with false bravado, unable to meet their eyes. "Virgil Earp deserves whatever he got! That sorry asshole never even give us a chance that day."

Stilwell flashed a mouthful of brownish teeth. "Same song, second verse."

"Damn if it ain't," Brocius agreed. "Wyatt's the kingpin of that bunch, and don't you never forget it, Ike. He just used Virgil's badge to give him a license to kill."

"If that's so," Finn ventured, "then we shore as hell gunned down the wrong man."

"Quit your bellyachin'!" Brocius yelled. "We're gonna get'em all. Every last one!"

Finn hawked and spat a wad of phlegm in the direction of the stove. "How d'you figger to do that?"

"I'm thinkin' on it."

"You been thinkin' on it near about three months. So far, all we've done is wing Virgil. That ain't much to show for what's owed us."

"Why, hell, Finn," Stilwell chortled. "We stole better'n four hundred head of cows and robbed a stage. We sure as the dickens ain't done ourselves no harm."

"That's what I mean," Finn bridled. "We been runnin' around like a fart in a bottle. Half the time we're down in Mexico rustlin' cows and the other half we're in some greaser cathouse tryin' to catch a dose of clap. That ain't gettin' the Earps killed."

"We'll kill'em!" Brocius said viciously. "Wyatt Earp's on the top of my list! So don't you worry your head about it, Finn. You hear me?"

"Yeah, I hear you."

"C'mon, Finn." Ike nudged his brother in the ribs. "Don't act so down in the mouth. Bill ain't never led us wrong yet, has he? He'll get it figgered out."

"I never said he wouldn't. I'm just askin' when."

"I'll tell you when!" Brocius exploded. "When I'm gawddamn good and ready! Anybody put your brains in a jaybird and the sonovabitch would fly backwards."

"What the hell's that supposed to mean?"

"It means you're dumber'n a horseturd! Don't you think Earp's on his guard now? Christ, he probably don't stick his nose outdoors after sundown. We've got to wait till he gets over the jitters! Then we'll nail his butt once and for all."

"How long's that gonna take?"

"Till I sayso and not a minute sooner."

"Well, don't take it personal, but I sure as shit ain't gonna hold my breath waitin'."

"You keep on and you're liable to be holdin' your breath a lot longer'n you think."

Stilwell waved them apart. "Simmer down! Bill's got the right idea, and no two ways about it. We just have to wait till Earp gets careless. It'll happen, don't never believe it won't!"

"You bet'cha!" Ike slapped his knee. "Catch the bastard when he ain't lookin' and blow him to Kingdom Come. I'd give a nickel to see his face when it happens!"

"How would you manage that?"

Ringo's question took them by surprise. Everyone stared at him a moment, then turned back to Ike. He shook his head, smiling lamely.

"I don't get you, Johnny."

"It's simple enough," Ringo said mildly. "How can you see a man's face when you shoot him in the back?"

"Aw, quit your funnin', Johnny."

"I'm not funnin'," Ringo said with exaggerated gravity. "Tell you the truth, I think Earp has a point."

"A point?"

"Yeah, about you boys being bushwhackers. Course, I guess he was feeling charitable and just overlooked the fact that you're not very good at it."

Stilwell laughed uneasily. "That's a helluva thing to say, Johnny."

"Simple statement of fact," Ringo remarked. "You boys can't even backshoot a man proper. Otherwise Virgil Earp wouldn't be flyin' on one wing."

There was a moment of oppressive silence. The men looked everywhere but at Ringo, trading sheepish glances. Then Brocius wormed around in his chair, hunching forward.

"You're talkin' out of turn, Johnny."

"What's the matter, Bill?" Ringo inquired. "Your ears burning?"

"Watch yourself," Brocius said stiffly, his lips white. "I don't let no man call me yellow."

"Why, Bill, I wasn't callin' you a coward. I just said you'd sooner backshoot a man than the other way round."

"You're so gawddamn tough," Brocius challenged him. "Whyn't you go face'em down your ownself?"

Ringo regarded him without expression. The other men waited, nervously watching the test of wills. Brocius knew he'd gone a step too far. He wondered if he could outdraw the muddy-eyed gunman, and realized he might very well die trying to preserve his leadership of the gang. His pulsebeat quickened, and the palms of his hands suddenly felt sweaty. He sat perfectly still, waiting.

Then, quite casually, Ringo rose to his feet. He walked to the door and opened it. On the verge of stepping outside, he turned and looked back over his shoulder. He fixed Brocius with a gallows grin.

"I think I'll take a ride into Tombstone."

Spearing his hat off a wall peg, he laughed and jammed it on his head. The sound of his laughter still filled the room when the door closed.

CHAPTER 10

"I still say it's damn queer."

"You're too antsy." Holliday wagged his head with a wry smile. "A backshooter pays no attention to the calendar. He's got all the time in the world."

"Well, I don't," Earp reminded him. "Brocius could hold off till doomsday, and it'd suit me just fine. But he won't, and we both know it."

"I think that newspaper article impressed you more than it did him. Anyone called you those names, you'd just naturally feel bound to face him down. Brocius isn't built that way, and there's the difference. He'll swallow his pride and wait for you to drop your guard."

"I wish to hell Virge was able to travel."

"He won't mend any faster with you in an uproar all the time."

"He damn sure couldn't mend any slower! We're like ducks in a shootin' gallery, and the odds get worse the longer we wait."

"All depends," Holliday grunted. "Your number

isn't up till it shows, and every day's a new toss of the dice."

Walking along Allen Street, the men fell silent. The earth swam in a bluish dusk, and high in the sky a fiery cloud blazed in the last rays of sunset. Ahead lay the Alhambra, and for all of Holliday's philosophical tone, there was nothing leisurely about their pace. These days, neither of them trusted the streets after dark.

Yet Holliday wasn't all that displeased with the situation. The worse the odds became, the more Earp needed him. Peace and tranquility would have weakened, perhaps even eliminated, that need. He much preferred the threat of imminent bloodshed.

Their friendship, from the start, had been one of mutual dependence. Holliday, despite his sullen manner, was not altogether misanthropic. No man ever completely purges himself of the need for human contact. Several years ago, at a low point in his life, he had latched on to Wyatt Earp in the way of a drowning man grasping at flotsam. Earp had accepted him as he was, seemingly unconcerned with his racking cough or his cynical outlook. At the time, Holliday thought it was perhaps his last chance to throw in with someone worthy of his respect. He was of the same opinion even now.

In exchange, he gladly allowed Earp to trade on his reputation as a mankiller. His presence alone, particularly here in Tombstone, served to enforce Earp's will on others. While one was cunning and ambitious, the other was a perfect assassin, ever eager to pull the trigger. Still, though they worked well together, they were alike only in their willingness to resort to violence. In all other things they were quite dissimilar.

Holliday was a Southerner, a man of breeding and education. Incurable tuberculosis had brought him West, seeking a drier climate. Even on the frontier, however, there was small demand for a dentist who coughed blood. Circumstance, and physical frailty, had led him into the life of an itinerant gambler. An ungovernable temper, coupled with that same physical frailty, had transformed him into a mankiller. In the truest sense, the Colt sixgun was for him the equalizer. He killed men simply because it was his sole means of defending himself. Then, too, he enjoyed the sport of wagering life against life. It gave a certain tang to an otherwise bleak existence.

By contrast, Wyatt Earp was a Yankee whose family had joined the westward migration. An uneducated farm boy, he had become a drifter with a yearning to better himself. His upward climb had taken him from buffalo hunter to sometimes peace officer to bunco artist and mining entrepreneur. He was coarse, by no means a gentleman, but he possessed a quick mind and a near infallible insight into the weaknesses of others. He killed men not for sport or some perverted sense of contest. He killed to protect what he'd gained, and the things he yet coveted.

Holliday understood all that. In fact, he understood Earp better than Earp understood himself. Tonight, he knew full well that Earp was torn between the urge to run—thereby removing his brothers from danger—and the need to revive his political fortunes in Cochise County. Holliday, whose loyalty was unswerving, would follow either way. Given a choice, however, he would have preferred to die fighting on the streets of Tombstone rather than succumb to the ultimate ravages of lung consumption. Having killed more than a score of men, he thought it would be the supreme irony if he ended up dying in bed. By no means a brave man, he was simply a fatalist who no longer feared death. For him, the hourglass was already down to a few grains of sand.

Nearing the Alhambra, he decided there was nothing to be gained in pressing the matter further. Earp was playing for time, clearly on the defensive. He wouldn't fight unless it was forced on him, and even that prospect left him badly troubled. Weighed in the balance, the safety of his brothers had assumed greater value than personal ambition. It seemed likely he would quit and run the moment Virge was able to travel. Whether he would return to fight another day was open to speculation. With Earp, anything was possible.

From downstreet, Holliday saw Jack Johnson approaching the Alhambra. He still considered the man a smalltime grifter, but he was accommodating and always good for a few laughs. Which was more than could be said for most of the cardsharks who frequented Tombstone's gaming parlors. Johnson flipped them a salute and halted, waiting outside the front door.

"Holliday!"

The shout stopped Holliday in his tracks. He turned and saw Johnny Ringo emerge from a doorway across the street. The streetlamps were already lit and Ringo's features were plainly visible. The corners of his mouth were twisted in a wolfish smile.

"I got a bone to pick with you, Holliday."

"Yeah?" Holliday said tonelessly. "What's that?"

"You're a double-dipped son-of-a-bitch, and a card cheat to boot."

Holliday's face went chalky. He was aware of Earp at his side, but his concentration was focused on Ringo. All in a flash, he weighed his chances and knew he couldn't beat the younger gunman in a fair fight. He still wasn't afraid to die, but he was reluctant to have it happen right now. A bigger fight was brewing, and he desperately wanted to stick around until then. Besides which, he told himself, Earp still had need of his gun. To go out now would be like leaving a friend in the lurch.

He spread his hands in a bland gesture. "Ringo, I'm not lookin' for trouble. Suppose we let it lay till another time?"

Ringo threw back his head and laughed. In the lamplight, he displayed a mouthful of teeth as square as sugar cubes. His hand hung loosely by the sixgun holstered on his hip.

"Trouble's found you, whether you're lookin' for it or not. I'm here to punch your ticket, Holliday!"

Starbuck remained motionless beside the door. He saw an evil light in Ringo's eyes, a steady, confident gaze that was at once striking and cold. Word had it that Ringo was the deadliest gunman in Arizona, and he could easily understand why. What he failed to understand was why Holliday would crawfish. To his knowledge, the gambler had never declined a challenge.

Abruptly, Earp turned and strode several paces down the boardwalk. His move effectively flanked Ringo, and brought everything to a standstill. When he spoke, his jaws were clenched so tight his lips barely moved.

"Ringo, I'd advise you to let it drop."

"Stay out of this!" Ringo shouted, biting off the words. *"It's between Holliday and me!"*

Earp's face was blank, as though cast in metal. "No dice! You'll have to take both of us."

"How about it, Holliday?" Ringo taunted. "You gonna let him fight your fight for you?"

"Why fight?" Holliday stalled. "I've got nothing personal against you. Our quarrel's with your back-shooter friends."

"Horseshit!" Ringo yelled in a loud hectoring voice. "We've got a score to settle and I'm callin' you out."

"Water over the dam," Holliday temporized. "Why don't I buy you a drink and let's talk about it?"

"C'mon!" Ringo said defiantly. "I always heard Doc Holliday couldn't be beat. Let's see you prove it!"

"No," Holliday slowly shook his head. "I aim to walk into the Alhambra and have that drink. You're welcome to join me."

"You four-flushin' bastard! Stand and fight!"

Starbuck saw a golden opportunity materializing before his eyes. Ringo would get Holliday, and Earp would get Ringo. One down on each side and then the killing would start in earnest. He waited, savoring the moment.

"Don't anybody move!"

Sheriff Behan and a deputy advanced along the boardwalk, guns drawn. So intent had Starbuck been on the deadly tableau before him that he hadn't seen them approaching. He cursed softly under his breath, all of his expectations suddenly spoiled. Then a random thought popped into his mind. Behan had attempted to intercede in the OK Corral shootout. Yet, despite his best efforts, three men had died that day. Perhaps tonight's opportunity wasn't lost after all.

"Drop your gunbelt!" Behan ordered. "Do it right now!"

Ringo turned his head just far enough to rivet the sheriff with a look. "Take a walk, Behan! This here's a private argument."

"Not tonight," Behan said, flicking a glance at Earp. "This time, I'm the only one wearin' a badge. You boys unload that hardware—pronto!"

Earp and Holliday were strangely silent. Watching them, Starbuck realized they would comply without protest. His hopes took another dive, then surged as his gaze shuttled to Ringo. The younger gunman's features were knotted in a brutish grimace.

"You're outta line!" he barked. "There's no law against us settlin' a personal dispute."

"Maybe not," Behan rejoined. "But there's a town ordinance against carryin' firearms. You just violated it and you're under arrest."

Holliday and Earp looked at him like he was crazy. Even his own deputy appeared somewhat uncertain.

Starbuck mentally crossed his fingers, still hoping.

"You're loco!" Ringo howled. "Everybody in this goddamn town packs a gun!"

"Tell it to the judge," Behan said bluntly. "You broke the law and that's that."

"Go to hell!" Ringo sputtered. "I don't hand over my gun to nobody!"

"I'll only warn you once more that you're under arrest."

"Stick it up your ass and sit on it!"

Behan motioned to his deputy. "Cover him! If he moves, shoot him dead."

The deputy brought his pistol to eye level, thumbing the hammer to full-cock. His arm was steady, and he centered the sights on Ringo's shirtpocket. Behan's cool stare bored into the fiery-tempered *pistolero*.

"Stubborn will get you killed! Drop that gunbelt and be mighty damn quick about it."

A taut silence fell between them. All up and down the street, miners and townspeople who had stopped to watch the affair swiftly scattered into nearby doorways. Ringo stood immobile, his eyes shifting from Behan to the snout of the deputy's pistol. At last, with a muttered curse, he unbuckled his gunbelt and let it fall to the ground.

Behan turned to Holliday. He held out a square, stubby-fingered hand. "I'll take your gun."

Holliday brushed his coat aside and unholstered an ivory-handled Colt. Extending it butt first, he jerked his chin at Earp. "Wyatt had no part in this. It was just me and Ringo."

"He's armed," Behan said deliberately. "That makes him an accessory."

"You've had your fun," Holliday warned him. "Don't get greedy."

Behan studied Earp a moment, debating with himself. Then he shrugged and glanced at Starbuck. "What about you, Johnson? Got any bright remarks tonight?"

"Nope." Starbuck squared himself up, grinning. "It's just like Doc told you, Sheriff. Wyatt and me was innocent bystanders."

"Careful, Johnson, or people will start callin' you the alibi-man."

Starbuck laughed. "Sticks and stones, Sheriff. No way to stop folks from talking."

"You still keep damn poor company."

Behan moved back a step, ordering Holliday and Ringo to precede him. Their eyes met in a hostile exchange, then they fell in alongside one another and marched off toward the jail. The deputy collected Ringo's gunbelt and hurried after Behan. A moment later, the little procession disappeared around the corner.

Starbuck looked sad. "Damn shame! Ringo's the one that started it, not Doc."

"C'mon," Earp grumbled. "I need a drink."

Starbuck followed him into the Alhambra. There was an empty space at the end of the counter, and Earp told the barkeep to leave the bottle. He knocked back a quick shot, then poured himself another round. Starbuck sipped, allowing the silence to build. His somber expression was genuine, without need of pretense. He was deeply resentful that the gunfight had been thwarted, bollixing what seemed a rare stroke of fortune. Yet he was alert to Earp's downcast mood. He thought to himself that something might still be salvaged from the night.

At last, with a violent oath, Earp slammed his glass on the bar. "Goddamn Harry Woods anyway!"

"Who?"

"Harry Woods," Earp said sharply. "That sawed-off little runt that prints the *Nugget*."

"Ooh yeah," Starbuck nodded wisely. "The one that ran that story."

"Story?" Earp rasped. "It was a death warrant! That's what brought Ringo out of his hole."

"Ringo?" Starbuck suddenly played dumb. "What's he got to do with anything?"

"Hell, he's one of the Brocius gang."

"So I've heard. But he came after Doc, not you."

"Yeah, so?" Earp conceded glumly. "What're you drivin' at?"

"Well, you said it was Woods' story that caused it. From where I stood, it sounded like Ringo's got something personal against Doc."

"Bad blood between 'em," Earp said vaguely. "Goes back a long ways."

Starbuck looked at him, unable to guess what might be going through his mind. He knew Earp was lying, and could only speculate as to the truth. An expression of idle curiosity on his face, he decided to probe a bit further.

"Must've been something mighty fierce. Took a real set of balls for him to brace both of you that way."

Earp was evasive. "I seem to recollect they had words over cards."

"Doc and Ringo?"

"You act surprised."

"I am," Starbuck deadpanned. "Doc generally plays poker with a better class of people."

"When we first got here there wasn't any better class of people. Doc used to ride over to Charleston when things got slow. That's where he met Ringo."

"Charleston?"

"Few miles west of here," Earp said woodenly. "It's a hangout for cowmen mostly. Doc could always find himself a pick-up game over there."

"Is that where your trouble with Brocius started?"

Earp stared down at his glass, tightlipped. "What makes you ask?"

"You said there was bad blood between Doc and Ringo. I just naturally figured that would get Brocius into the act."

"I suppose it did," Earp said without conviction. "I wish to hell he'd never met any of that crowd."

Watching him, Starbuck decided not to press too far too fast. Yet, even as they talked, the germ of an idea had taken root in his mind. It was an offshoot of his newspaper gambit, but he realized instantly that it had even greater potential. Somehow he had to bring the Earps and the Brocius gang together in a head-on clash. Not the hit and run tactics of bushwhackers and backshooters. An occasional assassination, even an incident such as tonight's confrontation, simply wasn't enough. It had to be total war, no quarter asked and none given. A bloodbath.

Starbuck took a chance. "I wonder if Brocius put Ringo up to making a play for Doc?"

"What gave you that idea?"

"I reckon you did. Or at least what you said about that newspaper story. It stands to reason Brocius and his boys will try to save face. So maybe Ringo was picked to get the ball rolling."

"I don't follow you."

"Seems pretty obvious," Starbuck said solemnly. "Brocius means to knock you off one at a time. Tonight was Doc's turn, only Ringo got too big for his britches."

"By God, I think you've got something there!"

"I'd bet on it," Starbuck assured him. "Course, it's none of my business, but if it was me, I'd take the play away from them."

"How would you propose to do that?"

"Simplest way on earth," Starbuck smiled. "Get them before they get you."

Earp regarded him thoughtfully a moment, then nodded. "Jack, you just gave me a helluva idea. It wasn't exactly what you intended, but it's a pip!"

"Oh, yeah? What's that?"

"I think it's time I got myself a badge." Earp's mouth curled in a sinister smile. "Way past time!"

CHAPTER 11

For the next few weeks Starbuck hung around the Alhambra like a forlorn ghost. He was moody and dispirited, and unable to come to terms with an elemental flaw in his strategy. He had once more underestimated Wyatt Earp.

Late one afternoon, he sat alone at a poker table. The lull before the evening rush had left the Alhambra virtually deserted. As he had every night for the past month, he was scheduled to take Alice to supper somewhere around six. With an hour or so to kill, and nothing better to occupy his time, he had stopped in for a couple of drinks. Now, with a hand of solitaire spread before him, he listlessly shuffled the cards. His gaze was abstracted, and almost mechanically, he laid the jack of diamonds on top of the queen of diamonds. He stared at the cards like a man peering disconsolately into an open grave.

February was half gone, and he was gripped by a leaden sense of defeat. The clarity of hindsight made his stomach churn, and the infernal waiting sawed on his nerves. He thought it one of life's greater ironies that he had been instrumental in bringing law and order to Arizona Territory. The grandest joke of all was that he had inadvertently transformed a shifty scoundrel into a sworn peace officer. Even now, somewhere south of Tombstone, U.S. Deputy Marshal Wyatt Earp led a posse in search of the Brocius gang. It boggled the mind, and left the sour taste of bile in his throat.

A month ago, only one day after the Ringo incident, Earp had disappeared from town. Three days later, he had returned with a badge pinned on his chest. Somehow, though he offered no explanation, he had managed to have himself appointed U.S. Deputy Marshal for the Tombstone District. It was all very mysterious, and to the consternation of his political opponents, it was also very legitimate. U.S. Marshal Crawley Dake, headquartered in Tucson, had administered the oath personally.

Half the town was dumbstruck, and the other half waited with anticipatory relish for the next act in what seemed a comedy of the bizarre. Sheriff John Behan, now reduced to second fiddle, stomped around town in a faunching rage. Earp's commission, being federal, superceded both local and county authority. He was the top lawman in all of southern Arizona. The balance of power, virtually overnight, had changed hands.

Starbuck, no less astounded than the townspeople, recognized it as a brilliant improvisation. For cool nerve and audacious conniving, it was unsurpassed. With one stroke, Earp had risen above public censure and given himself an enormous advantage over the Brocius gang. He loudly proclaimed that he was going to run the outlaws out of Arizona. Privately, he let it be known that dead or alive was not an issue. He intended to take no prisoners.

On all counts, Starbuck's plan had gone haywire. His purpose was to goad Earp into action, and thereby provoke open warfare between thieves. The upshot was that Earp had gone him one better, leapfrogging to a scheme that seemed not only outlandish but wholly improbable. Never in his wildest fancy would Starbuck have imagined such a brazen, and totally unpredictable, turn of events. Nor would he have conjured the unlikely twist that a private vendetta could so easily be spliced into a civic crusade. Even worse, he could have envisioned no outcome that would have left him sitting on his rump in Tombstone.

Yet there he sat.

Upon recovering from his initial shock, he had assumed Earp would ask him to join the posse. After all, it was his prompting that had suggested the scheme to Earp in the first place. He wasn't particularly thrilled with the idea, but as a member of the posse it would still induct him into the Earp clique. Once on the inside, he would simply adapt his plan to fit the new circumstances. Ultimately, by hook or crook, he would have emerged with Earp's scalp on his belt. It hadn't worked that way.

At no time, either by word or intimation, had he been invited to join the posse. Instead, Earp had sworn in Holliday and his younger brothers, Morg and Warren. Then, in a stunning piece of arrogance, he had imported two professional *pistoleros* from south of the border. Operating out of Nogales, Sherm McMasters and Texas Jack Vermillion were known throughout the southwest. They were hired guns, mercenaries available to the highest bidder, and their work was considered top drawer. Earp, expedient to the end, pinned federal badges on them. No mention was made of salary, but the arrangement was hardly a secret. John Clum published reports in the *Epitaph* that a "civic group" had placed a bounty of $1000 on Curly Bill Brocius.

Starbuck concluded that he'd overplayed the role of happy-go-lucky cardsharp. Earp liked him, even trusted him, but apparently considered him a lightweight when it came to gunplay. The marshal and his posse rode out of Tombstone the third week in January. Starbuck was left to contemplate the ashes of a plan gone awry.

Forced to wait it out, Starbuck had turned to Alice for comfort and diversion. His feelings about her veered wildly. He enjoyed her company and she raised his spirits, and her abandon in bed made the wait somewhat more bearable. Yet the other side of the coin disturbed him, and gave him pause. She was like a schoolgirl with her first crush, except it wasn't puppy love. She was hearing church bells and organ music. Worse, she kept dropping broad hints that clearly tagged him the bridegroom in her fantasy. He did nothing to encourage her, nor did he attempt to prick the bubble. He was genuinely fond of her, and more to the point, he couldn't afford to alienate his only potential witness. At night, when she lay snuggled in his arms, he often had difficulty reconciling one with the other.

His excuse, which he perceived as legitimate, was

the overriding goal of bringing Earp to justice. All the more so now that Earp was operating under the mantle of a badge. Through the Wells, Fargo agent in Tucson, he had learned that considerable pressure had been brought to bear on Crawley Dake, the U.S. Marshal. Apparently Earp had called in all his political markers in Tombstone. Tom Harris, one of the territory's power brokers, had pulled the necessary strings to secure Earp's appointment as Deputy Marshal. Harris, in turn, was aligned with the Tombstone businessmen who supported Earp. The link had been easily traced, and appeared to be little more than one hand washing the other. For all the quid pro quo, however, it posed a graver threat.

Brooding on it, Starbuck was of the opinion that Earp had raised his sights. Were he to rid Arizona of the Brocius gang, he would effectively kill two birds with a single stone. Foremost, and not to be discounted, was that he would eliminate the personal danger to himself and his brothers. At the same time, he would restore his own prestige, and emerge not just the man of the hour, but a lawman of imposing credentials. Using that as leverage, he could then consolidate his business alliances and move to gain control of Cochise County. It was a bold play and might very well succeed. By staking all his chips on the turn of a card, Earp could realize a complete turnabout in his political fortunes. From there, whatever venture he attempted, the sky would be the limit.

So far, Earp and his posse had produced little in the way of results. For the past three weeks they had chased around the territory without once sighting the outlaws. Clearly, Brocius and his gang had gone to ground, and were waiting for the dust to settle. There had been no more stage robberies, which pleased Wells, Fargo, and cattle rustling was reportedly at an all time low. But that in no way resolved the larger problem. Brocius and his gang, in the scheme of things, were merely a nuisance. Wyatt Earp was a dyed-in-the-wool menace.

The central question, Starbuck reflected, was how to bring the nuisance and the menace together. Slowly riffling the cards, he pondered ways to flush the gang from hiding and pit them in a bloodletting against the Earps. At this point, his options were limited and he was fresh out of ideas. He was also leery of creating any situation that might further Earp's resurgent flirtation with power. Yet anything was better than the Mexican standoff which now prevailed.

While it was no masterpiece, he still had one dodge left in his bag of tricks. Until now, he had hesitated using it simply because it was his last resort. If it failed, he would have nowhere to turn, and that prospect troubled him more than he cared to admit. Still, with the situation as it stood now, he was boxed into a corner anyway. From that viewpoint, there wasn't a hell of a lot to lose whatever he tried. Time was the enemy, and to sit on his butt any longer would be the worst mistake of all. What it boiled down to was the oldest axiom in the book. Nothing ventured, nothing gained.

He tossed the cards on the table and walked out of the Alhambra.

*   *   *

The sun dipped westward as Starbuck entered the front door of the *Epitaph*. John Clum was seated behind a desk littered with foolscap and newspaper tearsheets. His expression was somewhat harried, like a man battling several fires with only one bucket.

"Afternoon, Johnson."

"Afternoon, Mr. Mayor."

Clum brightened. He liked titles, and respect. "What can I do for you?"

"Wondered what the latest was on Wyatt. You heard anything?"

Clum's smile vanished. The sour look Starbuck received was not unexpected. It was no secret that Clum's fortunes had waned in the last six months. His association with Earp had provoked the wrath of both the town council and the voters. Barring a miracle, his political career had been consigned to the dung heap. Still worse, the *Epitaph* was steadily losing subscribers and advertisers to Harry Woods' *Nugget*. His financial position bordered on the perilous, and there were rumors he had mortgaged his home to raise operating funds for the newspaper. His frown was that of a weary and troubled man at the end of a long day.

"The last I heard of Wyatt, he was down around Bisbee somewhere. That was almost a week ago."

"If he'd caught up with Brocius, I suppose you would've got wind of it by now?"

"Probably so," Clum said dully. "News like that would travel fast."

"Bisbee?" Starbuck appeared thoughtful. "You reckon Brocius and his bunch skipped into Old Mexico?"

"I wouldn't hazard a guess."

"Seems logical, though, doesn't it?"

Clum shrugged indifferently. "Who cares where they've gone? It's hardly front page news."

Starbuck lit a cheroot and stuck it in his mouth. Then he hooked his thumbs in his vest, puffing cottony wads of smoke. "I've been thinking on that very subject, Mr. Mayor. The way it looks to me, it's high time Wyatt got the credit he deserves."

Clum looked startled. Like everyone else in town, he knew that the gambler named Johnson was practically a member of the Earp family. Alice Blaylock's visits to his hotel room, coupled with the fact he'd attached himself to Earp, had set the gossip mill churning. Yet, for all that, Clum knew he was considered something less than a mental wizard.

"Exactly what credit do you think Wyatt deserves?"

Starbuck ticked it off on his fingers. "There hasn't been a single stage robbery since he took out after Brocius. None of the mines have reported a payroll holdup. And there's talk that rustled cows are scarcer than hen's teeth. I'd say Wyatt has kept his promise, and he's done it in spades."

"You seem to forget he hasn't caught Brocius."

"Strictly beside the point," Starbuck said confidently. "He's put the Brocius gang out of business, probably scattered them to hell and gone across the border." He paused, using his cheroot like a wand, and scrolled a headline in the air. "Wyatt Earp has brought law and order to Arizona Territory!"

"You're right!" Clum marveled. "By all that's holy, he has done it, hasn't he?"

"See?" Starbuck grinned. "You hadn't thought of it that way and likely no one else has either. You stick that on your front page and they'll probably give Wyatt a medal. Might even erect a statue to him!"

Clum considered that unlikely. But the gist of the idea was sound, and anything that enhanced Earp's image would work to his own benefit as well. Elbows on the arms of his chair, he steepled his fingers and stared off into space.

"I like it." His voice was reverent, almost a benediction. "U.S. Deputy Marshal Wyatt Earp brings law and order to Arizona Territory. By the saints, that'll make them sit up and take notice! And it's true. Do you realize that, Johnson—it's indisputably true!"

"Gospel truth," Starbuck affirmed. "The town idjit could see that."

Clum grabbed a sheet of foolscap and began writing furiously. Starbuck flicked an ash with his pinky finger and crammed the cheroot back in his mouth. He looked proud as punch.

Shortly after dark, Starbuck slipped through the back door of the *Nugget*. While he waited in the print room, Harry Woods drew the shades on the front windows. Then he walked forward and took the wooden armchair beside Woods' desk.

"I just had a chat with your competition."

"Our esteemed mayor?"

"Prize sucker," Starbuck said quickly. "Nobody's easier to gaff than a man with larceny in his blood."

Woods smiled. "Tell me about it."

"I conned him into running a story on how Earp

has tied a can to Brocius' tail. He thinks he's beating the drum for Earp, but that's pure whiffledust. What it'll really do is make Brocius mad enough to chew nails."

"You are, indeed, a devious man."

Starbuck chuckled softly. "Harry, this time we'll pull out all the stops. I want you to publish those two lists, side by side. On the left side, a list of the dates the stages were robbed. On the right side, a list of the dates Earp purchased property. No editorial comment, just the lists by themselves. Let folks draw their own conclusions."

Woods studied him with admiration. "I daresay Brocius and Company will find that fascinating reading."

"I'm depending on it," Starbuck nodded. "If they're like most outlaws, they spend it as fast as they steal it. I'm betting they don't own much more than the clothes on their backs."

"Yet Earp, by contrast, is worth a fortune."

"In addition to which, he's kept them on the run for nearly a month. No holdups, no rustled cows, nothing. The way they look at it, he's taking the bread out of their mouths."

"Not to mention the fact that he's doing his level best to kill them."

"One more thing," Starbuck added. "I want you to write an editorial blasting Earp. Something to the effect that he doesn't give two hoots in hell about ridding the territory of outlaws. Charge him with using the Brocius gang to his own political ends, turning their skeletons into steppingstones. I think you get the general idea."

"Indeed, I do!" Woods laughed. "You intend to rub their noses in it. The *Epitaph* story, the lists, my editorial! Brocius and his men won't be able to ignore all that. They'll go off like skyrockets!"

"If they don't," Starbuck said ruefully, "I'll be in a helluva fix, Harry. I'm just about at the end of my string."

"Never fear, Luke! The pen is mightier than the sword . . . especially a poison pen!"

Starbuck wasn't fully convinced. But, then, as he'd told himself earlier, he had nothing whatever to lose by trying. He left Woods scribbling with a sort of mad glee over an impassioned editorial.

Starbuck knew something was wrong the moment she opened the door. Alice's smile was bleak, and she looked wretched. Stepping inside, he found Earp seated in the parlor. He stopped, genuinely surprised, then crooked his mouth in a jack-o'-lantern grin.

"Well, knock my socks off! Where'd you come from?"

"Just rode in, not more than ten minutes ago."

"You got'em!" Starbuck hopped toward him like a dancing bear. "I know you! You wouldn't have quit unless you got'em."

Earp gave him a hangdog look. "No such luck. We never even got a sniff."

"I'll be switched," Starbuck said, suddenly somber. "You mean to say they got away—clean?"

"That's about the size of it."

"So what's next? You aim to rest up a spell and then head out again?"

"Jack, I wouldn't have the least goddamn idea where to look. We've combed the territory from stem to grudgeon, and it's like they dropped through a hole in the ground."

Starbuck glanced at Alice and she ducked her head toward the door. She quite obviously wasn't pleased by her brother-in-law's return. For his own reasons, Starbuck was none too happy himself. After nearly two months of effort, he felt very much as though he'd just hop-scotched back to square one.

"Well, listen, we'll talk some more. Let me buy you a drink later and you can tell me the whole story."

"Maybe tomorrow," Earp begged off. "I'm so damn wore out my butt's draggin' the ground."

"Sure thing, Wyatt! Get yourself a good night's sleep and I'll see you tomorrow."

On the way out the door, Starbuck glanced back and got a shock. Earp looked whipped, somehow drained of resolve. Now, more than ever, the double-barrel newspaper blast represented a last ditch effort. Unless it brought Brocius into Tombstone, there would be no war. No bloodletting, and no end to the case.

A sudden black rage swept over him. He promised himself that wouldn't happen. Somehow, one way or another, it would end.

CHAPTER 12

"Ten ball in the corner pocket."

Starbuck leaned over the pool table. He stroked the cue stick with a practiced hand and cleanly sank the ten ball. The cue ball magically reversed itself, spinning backwards on the green felt, then rolled to a stop near the left hand side-pocket. The angle was perfect for his next shot, on the eleven ball.

"Would you look at that position? Talk about blind luck!"

Morg's tone was bantering, slightly envious. Standing nearby, he watched as Starbuck eyed the eleven ball. Earp and Holliday, who were seated on a bench along the far wall, exchanged a knowing glance. Spectators, and hecklers, they were having a good laugh at Morg's expense. No one spoke as Starbuck sliced the eleven into the side-pocket. Quickly, calling his shots without hesitation, he cleaned the table. When the fifteen ball dropped, he walked to the near corner pocket and extracted two ten-dollar bills. He kissed them, grinning at Morg.

"Tough break." He tucked the bills into his vest

pocket. "You had it sewed up till you missed the ten
ball. Care to try another game?"

"Watch yourself, Morg," Earp ragged him. "Jack's
liable to trim your wick."

Morg wasn't put out in the slightest. "Why, hell,
Wyatt, don't spoil it! I'm just stringin' him along so
he'll raise the stakes."

"Guess again," Holliday injected dryly. "You're the
one that's being hustled."

"Oh yeah!" Morg said with a wide peg-toothed
grin. "Well suppose we make it twenty a game, and
see who gets stiffed. How about it, Jack?"

"Suits me." Starbuck turned his head and gave Earp
a broad wink. "He thinks he's found himself a pigeon.
Reckon I've got a chance?"

"What you've got," Earp smiled, "is a gift for gab."

"Amen to that," Holliday added. "Get him started
and he'll talk the gold right off a man's molars."

While Morg racked the balls, Starbuck chalked his
cue and prepared to break. The pool table was located
in the rear of Hatch's Saloon. Benches lined the walls,
and an overhead lamp bathed the table in brilliant
light. A side door, with glass in the upper panel, led
to an alleyway. Up front, a crowd was ranged along
the bar. It was nearing midnight, and the murmur of
their conversation was sportive, well laced with liquor.

Starbuck dropped the four and the nine on the
break. Talking and shooting, he then ran the one
through the seven. The eight ball lay flush against the
rail, offering a difficult bank shot. He took a moment
to study the angle, and finally addressed the cue ball
with a great show of confidence. The eight ball zipped

across the table, caught the corner of the pocket, and bounced erratically to the far rail. His grin faded, and he gave the eight a look of raw disbelief. Morg laughed out loud, moving into position.

"Stand back, Jack! Gimme room!"

Stepping aside, Starbuck halted beside Earp and Holliday. They immediately began razzing Morg, who returned their jibes with vulgar good humor. No slouch on a pool table, he pocketed the eight ball with a double bank shot. The cue ball rolled into perfect position, and he took a vaudevillian bow. Then, calling his shots, he began running the table with methodical precision.

Watching him, Starbuck reflected on the vagaries of the detective business. Shooting a game of pool with Morg seemed somehow emblematic of his investigation to date. By all rights, he should have had them under lock and key—or dead and buried—long ago. Instead, he was still playing games. Pool tonight, poker last night, a masquerade every night. Unproductive, and seemingly endless, games.

In a swift flight of mind, he realized a month had passed since Earp's return to Tombstone. At the time, he'd been convinced that the stories in the *Epitaph* and the *Nugget* would force someone to take action. His bet was on Brocius, but he nurtured a glimmer of hope that Earp and his posse would again resume the chase. Events of subsequent days had proved him wrong on both counts.

Brocius and his band of outlaws had seemingly vanished off the face of the earth. It was now the middle of March, and for the past month there had been no depredations of any nature. No stage holdups, no payroll robberies, no reports of rustled livestock. Nor had the gang made any attempt on the lives of Earp and his brothers. There was speculation that they had retired to less hazardous pursuits somewhere in Old Mexico. But no one knew for certain where they were. On either side of the border, all was peaceful, uncommonly quiet.

For Earp's part, he basked in the light of revitalized public esteem. Even his detractors—Harry Woods in the forefront—were forced to admit he'd routed the outlaws. Considering the number of robberies and killings in the last two years, an entire month without violence was looked upon as nothing short of miraculous. John Clum, naturally, made the most of favorable circumstances. The *Epitaph* trumpeted Earp's prowess as a lawman in every issue. According to the headlines, Arizona Territory slept better because Tombstone's noblest citizen now wore a badge.

Starbuck, observing all this with a jaundiced eye, knew his instinct hadn't played him false. Earp, like any good grifter, was quick on his feet. Having gained the upper hand, he would now milk it to the limit. If the Brocius gang reappeared, he would strike a fresh trail and resume the chase amidst great public fanfare. If the outlaws had gone on to other endeavors, he would continue to claim credit for ridding the territory of a murderous band of desperadoes. Either way, he would be a strong candidate for sheriff when election time rolled around. Earp's star was definitely in the ascendancy.

All the more apparent, Starbuck reflected, was

Earp's complete switch in attitude. He no longer spent his days, and nights, looking over his shoulder. He plainly had come to regard himself as the hunter, not the hunted. Nor was there any likelihood that he would now make a run for it. Virge was all but recuperated, and for the past several weeks, he'd been fit enough to travel. Yet there was no mention of such plans, and it seemed logical to assume the idea had been shelved. The Earp family, quite obviously, intended to remain in Tombstone.

Starbuck thought Earp's assessment of Brocius was perhaps too optimistic. An outlaw might tuck tail and run for cover, but that made him no less dangerous. In Starbuck's experience, a backshooter was the most tenacious of all mankillers. Some perverted sense of pride, harnessed with an obsession for revenge, gave them extraordinary patience. He knew of instances where such men had waited for years, nursing a long-forgotten grievance, before they struck. He considered it very probable that Curly Bill Brocius was just such a man.

Still, there was no denying that Earp had a high opinion of himself these days. The tipoff was in little things, quirks of character. Not only did he smile, which was somewhat like watching granite crack, but he occasionally attempted a joke. Tonight, with business slow, he'd even suggested they quit early and take in the town. After catching the last act at the Birdcage Theatre, they had walked over to Hatch's Saloon for a nightcap. Morg, who fancied himself a pool shark, had challenged Starbuck to a game. The stakes were friendly, but Starbuck had taken inordinate pleasure in winning the first round. Lately, he hadn't had too much success in beating the Earps at anything.

Morg dropped the fourteen ball and stood back to survey the last shot. He was directly across the table, facing them, on line with the side door. As he chalked his cue, one of the saloon regulars, George Berry, walked back to have a look. Wobbling slightly, Berry appeared to be feeling no pain. He listed to a stop beside Holliday, and focused a bloodshot gaze on the pool table.

"I got four-bits says Morg makes it."

"Four-bits!" Morg laughed. "Bet your whole bank-roll, George. It's a lead-pipe cinch!"

"No, make it four-bits," Earp said humorously. "I'll cover it, and I wouldn't want George to go away busted."

"That's a helluva note," Morg said with a mocking smile. "You mean to say you'd bet against your own brother?"

"Why not?" Earp needled him. "You're getting ready to miss that shot. I can see it in your eyes."

"He's right," Starbuck chimed in. "You choked up last game, and that was before we doubled the stakes."

"Good try, but there's no way you'll talk me out of it. I couldn't miss that shot if my hands were tied! You and Wyatt just hide and watch."

Morg chuckled and stepped in behind the cue ball. The fifteen ball was opposite him, almost directly in line with the side-pocket. He dabbed chalk on the tip of his cue stick, and checked the angle one last time. Then he leaned forward over the table.

The upper panel in the alley door suddenly erupted

in a sheet of flame and shattered glass. The roar of
gunfire swept through the room like a drum roll. Morg
screamed and dropped the cue stick. His hands clawed
at empty air, then he fell on top of the pool table and
slowly crumpled to the floor.

Shots snicked across the room in a hailstorm of
lead. Earp and Holliday, miraculously unscathed, flung
themselves off the bench. All around them slugs thun-
ked into the walls and exploded the bench in a shower
of splinters. George Berry staggered, struck by a way-
ward bullet, and collapsed as though his legs had been
chopped off. In the same instant, Starbuck threw himself to the floor and rolled toward the end of the pool
table. A split-second later he rose to one knee, drawing
the Colt. He leveled his arm and thumbed three quick
shots through the alley door.

Then, as suddenly as it began, the firing ceased. A
haze of gunsmoke hung over the pool table and a
tomblike stillness descended on the room. For a moment, frozen in the eerie quiet, no one moved.

Starbuck broke the spell. Circling the pool table, he
crossed the room and flattened himself against the
wall. Then he jerked open the door and moved swiftly
into the alleyway. He crouched low, spinning in both
directions, the Colt extended and cocked. There was
nothing but darkness, and empty silence.

Turning, he stepped back through the door and
found Earp kneeling beside Morg. He glanced at Holliday, who was standing close by, and the gambler
slowly shook his head. His gaze dropped to Morg, and
he saw immediately that it was hopeless. The young-
ster had been hit several times, one of the slugs drilling

through his back and exiting high on his chest. His shirtfront was splotched with blood.

Morg groaned, his breathing rapid and uneven. His eyes focused on Earp and a trickle of blood seeped down his chin. The corners of his mouth lifted in a ghastly smile.

"Looks like my last game."

"Hang on," Earp muttered softly. "The doc's on his way."

"Funny." Morg blinked, casting his eyes about. "I can't see a damn thing."

A shudder swept over him and his mouth opened in a long sigh. One bootheel drummed the floor and his sphincter voided with a foul odor. Then he lay still.

Several moments passed in stunned silence. All the color leeched out of Earp's face and he stared stonily down at his brother. His face was blank, but his jaw muscles ticced as though he were trying to say something. At last, Holliday bent forward and placed a hand on his shoulder.

"He's gone, Wyatt."

Earp might have been deaf, for there was no response. His face became congested, and the veins in his temple knotted into purple ropes. He couldn't look away from the body.

"Wyatt." Holliday gently shook him. "It's no use. He's dead."

Earp seemed to awaken. He shrugged off Holliday's hand, took a deep breath and blew it out heavily. Almost tenderly, he reached down and closed Morg's sightless eyes. Then he climbed to his feet.

"Somebody get the undertaker. I want him looked after proper."

The night lay gripped in a mealy, weblike darkness. A clot of men stood watching from the saloon door. The undertaker and his assistant had already loaded Morg into the hearse. Now, carrying the shroud-wrapped body of George Berry, they crossed the boardwalk.

Some moments later, their task completed, they closed and latched the rear doors. Walking forward, they mounted the driver's seat from opposite sides. The undertaker gathered the reins and clucked to his team of matched coal black geldings. The hearse moved off upstreet and slowly disappeared into the night.

Under a nearby streetlamp, Earp stared after the hearse until it vanished. Then he turned to Holliday and Starbuck. His gaze shifted to the men crowded in the doorway, and he waited as they moved back inside the saloon. Finally, he glanced at Holliday.

"It's time to get Virge out of town."

Holliday nodded. "What about the women?"

"All of them except Mattie and Alice can go with Virge."

"You aim to leave them here?"

"No." Earp looked down and studied the ground a moment. "We'll find someplace to stash them in Tucson."

"Warren and Jim?"

"Jim goes with Virge and the women. Warren stays."

"It'll be tricky," Holliday said grimly. "No way to keep it a secret, and once word gets out, there's no tellin' what Brocius will try."

Earp reflected on it briefly. "We'll move 'em all at once," he said at length. "There's a westbound out of Tucson every evening. All we have to do is get them there in one piece and our worries are over."

"What then?"

Earp's eyes glazed with rage. When he spoke, the timbre of his voice was charged with malevolence. "Then we kill Brocius."

Starbuck felt his pulse skip a beat. There was a cold ferocity about Earp that he'd never seen before. The war he had tried in vain to provoke was about to start, and Earp's manner told him there would be no mercy asked nor none granted. He sensed it was time to act, or again get left behind.

"You'll need somebody to take Morg's place. I'd like the job."

Earp gave him a swift, appraising glance. "How many shots did you get off in there? Three, four?"

"Three," Starbuck said levelly. "Wish it'd done more good. By the time I got myself set, they'd already skedaddled down the alley."

"You did better than me and Doc."

"Not much," Starbuck hedged. "I didn't hit anybody."

Earp eyed him a moment. "Where'd you learn to handle a gun that way?"

"The hard way," Starbuck informed him. "The world's full of sore losers, and some of them take exception to the way I deal."

"All the same," Holliday interjected, "for a gamblin' man, you're still mighty sudden."

Starbuck smiled. "I hear you're pretty fast yourself, Doc. What makes you different from me?"

"No offense, Jack," Earp cut in quickly. "We're beholden for what you did tonight. But it's not your fight, and you'd likely be better off if we left it that way."

"Then let's just say I'm making it my fight. In case you forgot, Brocius and his boys were shooting at me too." Starbuck paused, looking from one to the other. "On top of that, I'm sort of interested in what happens to Alice. She'll tell you so herself, if you care to ask."

"Don't worry about her," Earp said with a trace of impatience. "She's family, and we take care of our own."

Starbuck played his hole card. "You haven't done so good up till now."

"What's that supposed to mean?"

"Last time out, Brocius gave you the slip six ways to Sunday. I'd say you need yourself a tracker."

Earp stared at him with puzzlement. "Are you tellin' me you're a tracker?"

"I've done my share."

"Whereabouts, just exactly?"

"Took lessons from California Joe. That was back in '67, with Custer, on the Wichita."

Holliday regarded him with squinted eyes. "You must've been the only scout in diddies."

"I'm older than I look," Starbuck said flatly. "Lots older in lots of ways."

He let the idea percolate a few moments. "What the

hell's the rub, anyway? You need another gun, and I'm willing to go along. You could damn well do lots worse!"

"Maybe so." Holliday's features were set in stubborn disapproval. "For my money, though, you're johnny-come-lately to this game."

"No, Doc, he's right," Earp said grudgingly. "Last time, Brocius ran us round and round in circles. Jack might just be the fellow we've needed all along."

"One thing's for certain," Holliday said stolidly. "He's a regular sackful of surprises."

"You tell me your secrets," Starbuck grinned, "and I'll tell you mine. Fair enough, Doc?"

"Let it lay," Earp silenced them. "Doc, get hold of McMasters and Vermillion. Tell them we ride at first light." He turned to Starbuck. "Jack, you hire a couple of buckboards from the livery. Have them at the house a little before dawn."

"Anything else?"

"Yeah," Earp said shortly. "Bring your gun. You're gonna need it."

CHAPTER 13

A streak of lightning forked the sky west of Tucson. Within seconds, the rumble of thunder sounded in the distance. The storm moved swiftly closer, somehow ominous in the lowering dusk.

A rented hack rolled through one of Tucson's seedier neighborhoods. The driver, one eye on the storm, popped his buggy whip, urging the team into a quickened pace. Up front, Warren and Mattie sat together in strained silence. Neither of them had spoken since the hack pulled away from the train station. No fool, she suspicioned she was being left behind, while the rest of the family went on to California. Earp had explained it away, telling the others he wanted her near. But she wasn't wholly convinced, and it showed. Her expression was one of heavy-hearted sorrow.

Starbuck, seated in the back with Alice, wasn't convinced either. Yet he thought it highly improbable that Earp would simply dump his wife. She, along with her sister, knew too much about his affairs in Tombstone. Still, they were being left behind, and that in itself raised intriguing possibilities. In the event Earp abandoned them, the fury of a woman scorned might very easily be turned to advantage. Wells, Fargo would then have two potential witnesses.

Alice held his hand in a death grip. She was frightened and confused, and clung to him as though terrified of the moment they must part. The news of Morg's death, he recalled, had unnerved the whole family. Their grief was heightened by the knowledge that their own lives were in jeopardy so long as they remained in Arizona. Their hasty departure from Tombstone, arranged in the dark of night, merely confirmed what no one dared say out loud. The Earp family was once more on the run. Stealing away, bag and baggage, like a caravan of gypsies.

In the early morning hours, with the sky still dark, the evacuation had gotten underway. Everyone had an assignment, and there was a sense of impending doom about the hurried preparations. Earp and Holliday, assisted by McMasters and Vermillion, had taken one of the buckboards to the funeral parlor. There, Morg's coffin was loaded aboard and lashed down with rope. Warren and Starbuck, meanwhile, got the rest of the family ready to travel. Virge and Jim, along with the six women, were dressed and waiting when Earp returned. The women were allowed only one carpetbag apiece, and even then, the buckboards were cramped and overcrowded. As false dawn lighted the horizon, the little caravan rolled north out of Tombstone.

Their immediate destination was Contention. A railway junction and freight yard, the small settlement lay some twelve miles north along the banks of the San Pedro. While the distance was not that great, it was a remote stretch of road, well suited to ambush. Earp, heedful of the danger involved, treated the operation somewhat like a military withdrawal. Outriders were assigned to the cardinal points. With himself and Holliday in the vanguard, Warren and Starbuck were posted on the flanks. The hired guns, Vermillion and McMasters, brought up the rear.

Starbuck had met the gunmen on several occasions during their stay in Tombstone. He recognized them as run-of-the-mill hardcases, a breed he held in low esteem. The border attracted many such men, quiet and cold-eyed, with little regard for the value of life. Their connection with Earp was somewhat of a mystery, never once alluded to in conversation. Yet they clearly respected Earp, and almost went out of their way to fawn over Holliday. It very much put Starbuck in mind of a wolf pack. There was a definite order of dominance, and while all were meat-eaters, those of lesser ferocity forever curried favor with the pack leader. He thought it entirely likely that they had all worked together before.

Around mid-morning, after an uneventful journey, they had arrived in Contention. From there, they caught the noon train, pulling into Tucson late that afternoon. Still under guard, the family was then herded into the depot, where they were to await the evening westbound. Warren, with Starbuck along for good measure, was assigned the task of locating a boardinghouse for Mattie and Alice. Outside the depot, Earp had handed Mattie a roll of money and allowed himself to be pecked on the cheek. Their parting was like some atavistic ritual, without emotion.

Now, less than an hour later, the hack rolled to a stop in front of a two-story structure that looked weather-beaten and in ill repair. The driver assured them it was clean and served decent meals, one of the few boardinghouses suitable for ladies. Warren jumped down and went inside to arrange accommodations. Starbuck helped the women from the hack, then unloaded the bags and carried them to the porch. On his way back to the street, Mattie passed him on the walkway. She seemed dazed, scarcely nodding when he spoke, and continued on into the house. Alice waited for him at the edge of the barren, weed-choked yard. She looked on the verge of tears.

"Cheer up!" he said lightly. "It's a little the worse for wear, but I'll bet they serve the best food in town."

Alice smiled wanly. "I wasn't thinking of that."

"Why so down in the mouth, then?"

"I was wondering—" Her eyes suddenly went misty. "Will I ever see you again, Jack?"

"Course you will," Starbuck assured her. "Once we get this business cleared up, I'll scoot on back here so fast it'll make your head swim."

"Promise?" she whispered, desperation in her voice. "I'd give anything in the world to believe you won't just . . . go away."

Starbuck was not a man who revealed his innermost thoughts. The girl was important to him, and not only as a potential witness. Over their months together he had developed a genuine affection for her, and he was concerned about her welfare. Yet old habits were hard to break, and in his business, emotions were something to be suppressed. He covered what he felt now with an offhand remark.

"Tell you what." He grinned, taking her by the shoulders. "You keep a light in your window. One of these nights I'll sneak up and blow it out, and we won't get out of bed for a whole week."

"Oh, Jack." She sniffed, blinking away tears. "You're terrible. You really are."

"Terrible good?" Starbuck cocked one eyebrow. "Or terrible bad?"

"You know very well." She bit her lower lip, silent a moment. Then she hugged him fiercely around the neck. "You will be careful, won't you? For my sake, please!"

"Why, you ought to know me better than that. Careful's my middle name! Don't worry your head on that score."

"I will," she said softly. "I'll worry every minute you're gone."

Warren appeared on the porch and came swiftly down the walkway. She pulled Starbuck's mouth to hers and kissed him soundly. Then she slipped past him, tears streaming down her face, and ran toward the house. He gave Warren a sheepish grin, lifting his shoulders in an elaborate shrug. Wordlessly, they climbed into the hack and seated themselves.

The silence lasted for several blocks. Starbuck's thoughts were on the girl, but he slowly became aware that Warren was staring vacantly into space. At length, after lighting a cheroot, he shifted around in his seat.

"Something bothering you?"

"What makes you think that?"

"For one thing, you look like you just lost your best friend."

"Maybe I did," Warren said miserably. "Mattie and me have always been pretty thick, up till now anyway. She sure gave me the dust-off back there. Wouldn't even say goodbye."

"That a fact?" Starbuck looked at him curiously. "I know she was partial to you, more so than your brothers anyhow. What's her problem?"

"Wyatt!" Warren burst out. "She's got some fool notion that Wyatt means to ditch her."

Starbuck's expression revealed nothing. "Hardly makes sense. Why would he want to get shed of Mattie?"

Warren averted his eyes, visibly troubled. "Lemme ask you something, Jack. You notice anything different about Wyatt . . . anything unusual . . . since last night?"

"I'm not exactly sure what you mean."

"I'm not either," Warren confessed. "But he's not himself. He's acting damn strange, and I can't rightly put my finger on it."

"Maybe it's Morg," Starbuck suggested. "He got hold of himself quick enough, but he took it awful hard when Morg died."

Warren shook his head. "I know Morg getting killed caused it. That's not what I'm talking about, though."

"You just lost me on the turn."

"It's—" Warren faltered, then rushed on. "Take a good look at his eyes. Maybe nobody except family would notice it, but it's there. Something mighty god-damn queer . . . spooky."

"Hold on now! Are you trying to tell me he's popped his cork?"

"No, I wouldn't go that far."

"Well, how far would you go?"

"I don't know, Jack. I just by God don't know!"

The storm broke shortly after nightfall. A blue-white bolt of lightning seared the sky and an instant later a thunderclap shook the depot. Then a torrent of rain struck the earth in a rattling deluge.

Already an hour overdue, the westbound pulled into town just as the storm unleashed its fury. A groaning squeal racketed back over the coaches as the engineer throttled down and set the brakes. The engine rolled past the depot and ground to a halt, showering fiery sparks in a final burst of power. The station agent, dressed in a rain slicker, walked forward as the conductor stepped down from the lead coach.

When the train stopped alongside the platform, Earp emerged from underneath the depot's over-hanging roof. He carried a double-barrel shotgun, and the shadowy figures ranged behind him were now armed with Winchesters. He slowly inspected the plat-form, watching intently as several passengers alighted from the train and hurried into the stationhouse. Then he turned his head and nodded.

Starbuck moved forward and took a position near the express car. A row of lanterns, strung along the front of the stationhouse, gave him a commanding view in either direction. Vermillion and McMasters

appeared from beneath the overhang, pulling a baggage cart which contained Morg's coffin. They trun-
dled the cart across the platform and jockeyed it into
position before the express car. A messenger threw the
door open, motioning with his hand. The gunmen
scrambled onto the cart, one on either end of the coffin, and carried it inside. Within seconds, they returned, jumping from the cart to the platform.
Collecting their Winchesters, they moved past Earp
and took up position at the far end of the depot.

Earp walked directly to the stationhouse door.
Opening it, he stuck his head inside, then turned and
moved back onto the platform. Holliday and Warren
came through the door, both of them armed with
Winchesters. Next out were Virge and his wife, trailed
closely by Jim and the other three women. They
splashed through the rain, led by Warren, and boarded
the middle passenger car. Earp took a last look around,
then followed them inside the coach.

Starbuck moved along the platform and joined Holliday. His coat was now soaked and rivulets of water
rolled off his hat as the rain continued in a steady
downpour. Through the car windows, he saw Earp and
Warren getting the family settled and stowing their
luggage in overhead racks. Watching them, he recalled
the concern expressed earlier by Warren. Since returning to the station, he'd observed Earp more closely,
and the change, though not pronounced, was evident.
Earp looked drawn, older than his years, and there was
a strange feverish cast to his eyes. Moreover, he was
quiet, uncannily quiet. All evening he had roamed the
station, avoiding conversation, curiously withdrawn.

He somehow reminded Starbuck of a mad bull hooking at cobwebs. A bull spoiling for a fight.

Some time later Earp and Warren stepped out the coach door. Their faces were somber, and it was clear their final goodbyes had been difficult. Earp glanced around the depot, then looked at Holliday.

"Everything all right out here?"

"So far." Holliday extracted a telegram from his inside coat pocket. "This came over the wire from Clum while we were in the waiting room. I figured it was best to wait till Virge and Jim were set before I showed it to you."

Earp scanned the telegram, then grunted. "Coroner's jury returned a verdict naming Pete Spence, Frank Stilwell and Florentino Cruz as Morg's killers. Wonder how they managed to overlook Brocius?"

Holliday knuckled back his mustache. "Well, at least we've got some names and a legal indictment. It's a place to start."

"Indictment, hell!" Earp tapped the marshal's star pinned on his coat. "All I need's this badge and a reasonable gun range. Let somebody else worry about the legalities."

Warren cleared his throat. "You still aim to kill 'em outright?"

"Why?" Earp asked with a clenched smile. "You got a better way?"

"Nooo," Warren said slowly. "Let's just make it look like they put up a fight. Otherwise it'll give Behan an excuse to swear out another murder warrant against us."

"Not a bad idea! Johnny Behan's one man I'd enjoy throwin' down on."

Earp's eyes strayed to the front of the train. A lightning bolt illuminated the sky and he suddenly stiffened. The figure of a man darted from behind a stack of railroad ties and ran across the tracks, disappearing around the front of the engine. Earp rapped out a sharp command.

"Doc, you and Warren stay here! Don't let anyone else on board. The rest of you come with me!"

Vermillion and McMasters rushed forward, trailing Starbuck, and they followed him down the platform. Earp led them around the caboose and across the tracks. Ahead, through the rain, they saw a man moving toward them, rising every few steps to peer in the coach windows. Then, glancing in their direction, the man spotted them and whirled to run. Earp threw the shotgun to his shoulder.

"Halt! Or you'll get it in the back!"

The man stopped and eased around with his arms in the air. As they approached him, the light from the coaches clearly outlined his features. He stared at them with a mixture of fear and bravado. Earp halted and slowly cocked both hammers on the scattergun.

"Stilwell, I know you're not alone. You've got about three seconds to tell me who's with you and where they are."

Stilwell swallowed hard. "You've got nothin' on me, Earp. There's no law against walkin' the tracks."

"Cut the bullshit! Talk quick or I'll dump both loads of this greener in your balls and let you die slow."

"Wyatt!"

Holliday rounded the caboose and hurried toward them. "We just saw Ike Clanton run around the corner of the station. Happened too fast to get a shot at him."

"That figures," Earp said over his shoulder. "Ike never was one to stick around for a fight."

Holliday halted beside him. "Who you got here?"

"Frank Stilwell." Earp grinned, turned his head slightly. "He obliged us by showin' up just when we heard he helped kill Morg."

Starbuck was startled by the expression on Earp's face. He saw there a wild homicidal rage, and deep within the ice-blue eyes, a look of feral savagery. Suddenly the engine chuffed smoke and the wheels groaned as the train got underway. Earp turned back to the outlaw, and there was a quiet steel fury in his voice.

"Stilwell, if you've got the faith, you better start prayin'. Your time's run out."

The train jolted forward and the first passenger car slowly rolled past them. Out of the corner of his eye, Starbuck saw the conductor and several passengers peering out the coach window. Then Earp triggered both barrels and the shotgun belched a yard-long streak of flame. Stilwell staggered backwards, the entire front of his coat blown apart. His knees suddenly buckled and he struck the ground hard, sprawled in a welter of blood.

The coaches gathered speed, and intermittent light from the windows framed Stilwell's face in a death-mask. Powder flash from the shotgun had set his clothes afire, but the rain quickly extinguished the flames. Wisps of smoke continued to rise from his blood-scorched body as the express car rattled past. Then the train was gone and a moment later the tail lights of the caboose were obscured by the storm.

Warren ran across the tracks. A jagged streak of lightning split the darkness, and he stopped, looking down at the body. His eyes widened, and he quickly turned away. After a moment he found his voice.

"Frank Stilwell?"

"Used to be," Holliday said without expression. "Now he's nobody."

"Better get used to it," Earp said gruffly. "You'll see lots more like him before we're through."

"Yeah," Warren mumbled. "I know."

Earp broke open the shotgun. He extracted the spent shells and contemptuously tossed them on the smoldering body. His mouth worked at the corners, and he stared down with an unsettling gaze, deep and intense. Several moments passed, then he laughed a low, gloating laugh.

"At least the sorry bastard didn't beg."

A cone of silence enveloped the men. Warren exchanged a worried glance with Starbuck, and a message passed between them. Unbidden, almost unwittingly, they were both thinking the same thing. The laugh they'd just heard was sane and yet somehow spooky. The laugh of a man skittering very near the edge of reason.

"Let's go," Earp ordered abruptly. "We've still got a long haul, and it won't all be this easy."

The men fell in behind Earp as he walked toward the depot. Lagging back, Starbuck looked at the body one last time. He smiled, telling himself it had begun and knowing in the same thought where it would end. The place where Frank Stilwell would soon take up residence.

The boneyard.

CHAPTER 14

Early the next evening Earp convened a council of war. The meeting had been called at Starbuck's suggestion, the purpose being to work out strategy for the upcoming manhunt. Apart from Holliday, no one else was asked to attend.

The others, Warren and the two hired guns, raised no objections. The previous night, after Stilwell's killing, Earp had led them on a long walk to the first flag station outside Tucson. From there, they hopped a freight train to the railway junction at Contention, and then traveled by horseback to Tombstone. The party had arrived, weary and trailworn, shortly after the noon hour. None of them had slept since day before yesterday, and the tension of the last forty-eight hours had sapped their energy. Earp took rooms at the Occidental, and the men had fallen gratefully into bed. Holliday and Starbuck were awakened before suppertime, and had joined Earp in the hotel diningroom. The others were left to their own devices for the balance of the night.

At Starbuck's request, Earp had obtained a detailed

map of Arizona Territory. Now, huddled around the desk in Earp's room, they examined the map closely. Starbuck, by virtue of his hitch as an army scout, asked the questions.

"Last time out, where did you start?"

Holliday stabbed at the map with a bony finger. "Charleston."

"Why there?"

"Because that's where Brocius and his boys hang out."

"Any special reason?"

"There's a saloon—The Silver Dollar—that caters to cattlemen and their hired hands. Brocius only rustles cows down in Mexico, so the welcome mat's always out. He sells cheap and there's plenty of ranchers that don't mind turning a crooked dollar."

"What made you think you'd find him there?"

"That's a damnfool question!" Earp's tone was hotly defensive. "Doc just told you why."

"I'm no lawman," Starbuck replied, suppressing a smile, "but it never hurts to put yourself in the other fellow's boots. Virge had just been bushwhacked, and Brocius probably figured you'd come looking for him. Way it worked out, he knew right where you'd start."

Earp digested the thought, nodding. "You're sayin' we won't find them in Charleston this time either."

"That's about the size of it."

"So where do we start?"

Starbuck warded him off with upraised palms. "Let's take it step by step. After Charleston, where did you look next?"

"Everywhere," Earp grumbled. "We hit the Clanton

ranch that same day. Then we rode southwest." He traced the route on the map. "The Huachuca Mountains and a swing along the border. Up to Bisbee and across to the Dragoons and Benson. Then we circled back to the border and kept on circlin'. Before it was over, I felt like a dog chasin' his tail."

"All that time," Starbuck asked, "didn't you ever once cut their sign?"

"Hell no!" Earp said bitterly. "Why do you think I finally called it quits?"

"You have to remember," Holliday interjected, "we're the outsiders around here. Brocius has friends all through the southern part of the territory. Nobody would give us the time of day, much less a tip on his whereabouts."

Starbuck took a moment to light a cheroot. He puffed thoughtfully, studying the map for a long while. At last, he grunted to himself and blew a plume of smoke into the air.

"Here's the way it looks to me. Charleston's out, and I'd say the same thing goes for the Clanton ranch."

Earp eyed him keenly. "You don't think they'd have gone back there after killin' Morg, is that it?"

"No, I don't," Starbuck said equably. "Even if they had, they would've been long gone by now."

"I don't get you."

"Ike Clanton took off last night like his pants were on fire. By now, they know Stilwell's dead and they know you aren't."

"Aren't what?"

"Dead," Starbuck said simply. "They were after you last night, not Virge. Probably three or four of them spotted around the depot waiting for a clear shot. Stilwell got careless and tipped their hand. That's why Clanton lit out so fast."

A puzzled frown appeared on Holliday's face. "You've sure got the voice of experience for somebody that's no lawman."

Starbuck regarded him with an expression of amusement. "Doc, you get the same experience on the other side of the fence. Stays with you longer, too."

"How so?"

"Because you live and learn, or you don't live at all."

"Judas Priest," Holliday said scornfully. "You're a cardsharp, and you served with Custer, and now you tell us you rode the owlhoot. You're a regular jack-of-all-trades, aren't you?"

"After a fashion." Starbuck's smile broadened. "Course, that don't necessarily mean I'm the master of none."

"The way you talk, you know a damnsight more than you ever let on before."

"Hold on, Doc." Earp gave him a reproachful look. "The way he talks makes sense. Damn good sense!"

"That's my point," Holliday countered. "Ever since we met him, he's been playin' the fool. Now, all of a sudden, he's not as dumb as he acts. I don't like it."

Starbuck sensed danger. A cynic was always suspicious of change, and Holliday's skepticism might very well prove contagious. He grinned, the cheroot clamped between his teeth, and put on a bold front.

"Doc, let me tell you something, one grifter to another. I choose my friends real careful, and even then,

I wait a long time to let them know I'm swifter than I look. That's a lesson I learned the hard way, and it's brought me through many a tight scrape."

He paused, staring Holliday directly in the eye. "Now, if that rankles your fur, then it's me that misjudged you, not the other way round. You just say the word, and I'll go on about my business. Adios and no hard feelings."

The bluff worked. Earp gave Holliday the fish-eye, warning him to carry it no further. Then his glance shifted quickly to Starbuck.

"Doc didn't mean nothin', Jack. The last couple of days, you've just showed us more than we bargained for, that's all."

"No offense taken." Starbuck rocked his hand, fingers splayed. "I just tend to get serious when the killing starts."

"Who don't?" Earp said agreeably. "Now, suppose we get back on track. You never did say exactly where you figured we ought to start."

"It's all guesswork," Starbuck said earnestly, leaning over the map. "Just the same, it looks to me like there's two possibilities. First, Brocius and his boys could've made a beeline for Mexico. Offhand, though, I'd say that's the least likely."

"Why?"

"Because McMasters and Vermillion work out of Nogales. They're old timers down that way, and Brocius probably figures they'd get wind of it if he showed up below the border."

"What's your second guess?"

"I think Brocius has a hideout somewhere pretty

close to home. Matter of fact, I'd be willing to bet that's where he holed up the last time you went after him."

"So where do we start?"

"The Clanton ranch."

"Some tracker!" Holliday shouted. "You just got through tellin' us they wouldn't go anywhere near the ranch."

"They won't, but I'd be awful surprised if they just rode off and left the place to run itself."

"That's right!" Earp verified. "Last time we was by there, they'd left the cook to look after things."

"Did you question him?"

"Why hell yes! We're not that stupid, Jack."

"I take it he didn't tell you anything."

"What's there to tell?" Earp said sternly. "I damn near broke his arm off, but he didn't know nothing about nothing."

"He knows one thing."

"Yeah, what's that?"

"Unless I'm way wide of the mark, he knows which direction they rode."

"Are you sayin' you can track 'em just by knowin' which direction they took?"

"That many horses," Starbuck reminded him, "leave a ton of tracks. Ton of horseshit, too. Show me the way they went and I'll follow them clean to hell."

"By God, you're not jokin', are you?"

"I've got an idea the joke'll be on Brocius this time."

"You sound mighty—" Holliday began, but there was a knock on the door, and he stopped.

"We're busy," Earp called. "Come back later."

"Wyatt!" The voice was muffled, and the knock more insistent. "It's John Clum. I have to see you!"

Earp muttered something to himself, then nodded. Holliday rose, moving to the door, and admitted Clum. The mayor rushed into the room, scarcely glancing at Starbuck. His expression was harried and a sheen of perspiration covered his face.

"Wyatt, we've got trouble, big trouble."

Earp waved him to a chair. "What's wrong now?"

"There's a warrant out for your arrest."

Earp stared at him, dumbstruck. Clum doffed his hat, tossing it on the desk, and dropped into a chair. He took out a handkerchief and wiped his face. His hands were trembling.

"A wire just arrived authorizing Johnny Behan to arrest you on sight. Fortunately, the telegraph operator owes me a favor, and he brought the wire to me first. I got him to hold off an hour before he delivered it to Behan."

"Warrant?" Earp asked in a froggy voice. "On what charge?"

"Murder," Clum said gravely. "The sheriff in Tucson had that westbound train stopped in Prescott. He got depositions from the conductor and several passengers. They identified you and Doc."

"By God, that takes gall! I'm wearin' a badge and Frank Stilwell was a wanted man. Where the hell does anybody get off chargin' me with murder?"

"It won't wash." Clum's tone was severe. "Those people say you executed Stilwell. All of them testified that he had his hands in the air, that he'd surrendered."

"He was wanted!" Earp said angrily. "Wanted for murder!"

"Wyatt, you're the wanted man now. You killed him like a hog in a charnel house, and there are eyewitnesses that will swear to it."

"I've still got this badge, and anybody—Behan included—will think a long time before they tangle with a deputy marshal."

"You were a deputy," Clum said hesitantly. "The U.S. Marshal revoked your commission late this afternoon. That was in the wire, too."

Earp shook his head violently. "We've still got connections! There's people that owe me, owe me plenty. We'll get'em to put in the fix and have it hushed up."

"Not for murder, they won't. Face up to reality, Wyatt! Once word gets around, all of them will wash their hands of you. You won't even exist so far as they're concerned."

"They owe me!" Earp said, almost shouting. "I've been their goddamn lightning rod in this town. It was me that done the dirty work and they better not forget it!"

"For your own good," Clum persisted, "you're the one that better forget it. Politics is a rotten business, and I shouldn't have to tell you that. Killing Stilwell was the last straw, Wyatt. You're a liability to them now, and they won't lift a finger to help you."

"They're tarred with the same brush! Either they help me or I'll take'em down with me."

"It's too late for that," Clum patiently explained. "We're talking about murder, not politics. You might smear their reputations, but what would that accomplish?"

Earp's mouth hardened. "It'd blow their plans sky high! Once I got done spillin' the beans, they wouldn't be able to show their faces in Cochise County."

"On top of which," Holliday said sullenly, "I'd make it my personal business to give every one of the sonsabitches a dose of lead poisoning."

"Doc, please!" Clum sputtered. "Killing them won't solve anything. You'd only make matters worse."

"I ought to start with you," Holliday said in disgust. "Way it looks to me, you're the first rat off the ship."

Clum suddenly appeared shaken, rigid with fear. "Good God, why won't you listen? I didn't have to come here tonight, and there's nothing in it for me one way or the other. I'm trying to convince you to save yourselves."

"We beat a murder rap once before," Earp told him. "Hell, they had us up on three counts that time."

"You won't beat this one," Clum said, voice low and urgent. "In Tucson, you wouldn't have a friendly judge sitting on the bench. You wouldn't even get a fair shake, much less an under-the-table deal. The case would go to trial and you'd be convicted. You know I'm right, too."

He paused, emotionally drained, and lowered his eyes. "You're through in Arizona, Wyatt. You have to get out as fast as you can ride. Otherwise, you'll wind up at the end of a hangman's rope."

A thick silence settled in the room. Earp rose and paced to the window. He stood there a long time, staring thoughtfully down at the street. At last, with a heavy sigh, he scrubbed his face with his palms. When he turned around, he permitted himself a grim smile.

"I never much cared for Tombstone anyway."

Starbuck marked again that his smile was a strange and chilling sight. It was more on the order of a rictus, some outward grimace that creased his mouth but never touched his eyes. Watching him, Starbuck briefly considered attempting an arrest, here and now. Then he put the impulse aside. Not only was he outnumbered, but he had no real faith in a judge and jury. He told himself there was a better way. A way that might still get Earp killed.

"You fooled me," Starbuck said casually. "I never would've pegged you as a quitter."

"*Quitter!*" Earp flared. "What the hell you mean by that?"

"Unless I heard wrong, you just got through saying you're pulling out of Tombstone."

"So?"

"So I didn't figure you'd let Brocius off the hook, that's all."

"You figured right," Earp said firmly. "I'm callin' it a day in Tombstone, but nothing else changes."

"You're not leaving?" Clum asked anxiously. "I beg you to reconsider, Wyatt. Another day in the territory may be one day too long."

"I'll leave when my business is finished. Not before."

"Then there's a very good chance you'll get yourself killed instead of Brocius. With a warrant in his pocket, Johnny Behan has you right where he wants you. He'll deputize every two-bit gunman in town, and do his level best to bring you back draped across a horse."

"You always were a worrywart, John. Have a drink and calm your nerves. Behan's the least of my troubles."

"I hope you're right. I genuinely hope so."

Earp's gaze moved to Starbuck. "Jack, hustle on down to the livery and boot somebody in the ass. Get our horses saddled and bring'em on back here *muy pronto*."

"We're pulling out tonight?"

"That's the general idea," Earp nodded, turning quickly to Holliday. "Doc, go roust Warren and the boys. Tell'em we ride in half an hour."

Starbuck and Holliday hurried from the room. When the door closed, John Clum was slumped in his chair, staring blankly at nothing. Earp, after folding the map into a neat square, got busy packing his saddlebags.

A short time later Earp descended the stairs to the lobby. His saddlebags were thrown over his shoulder and the sawed-off shotgun was tucked under his arm. Clum was beside him, and at the bottom of the stairs, they shook hands. Then he walked toward Holliday and the men, who were waiting near the front door.

"Everything ready?"

"All set," Holliday noted. "Horses are outside."

Earp led the way onto the veranda. The men trooped along behind him, moving in a tight phalanx to the hitch rack. There they mounted and sat watching him while he shoved the shotgun into the saddle scabbard. As he tied down his saddlebags, a voice suddenly sounded from upstreet.

"Earp! Wyatt Earp!"

Behan, flanked by a deputy, stepped off the boardwalk and rushed toward them. He halted a few paces away, darting a nervous glance at the men.

"Earp, I want to see you."

"Behan, if you're not careful, you'll see me once too often."

Behan squared himself up. "It won't do you any good to run. I've got a warrant for your arrest, and I'll be on your trail in the morning with twenty or thirty men."

"You do that." Earp's tone was icy. "We'll be lookin' for you."

Earp swung aboard his horse and reined sharply away from the hitch rack. The others brought their mounts around and rode off down the street. At the corner, where they turned west, Starbuck glanced back toward the hotel. He saw Behan throw his hat to the ground, then kick at it in an outburst of temper. Somehow, though he understood the lawman's frustration, it seemed a fitting end to his long stay in Tombstone.

He laughed and feathered his horse in the ribs.

CHAPTER 15

The dawn sky was metallic, almost colorless. The men were crouched low in an arroyo, their eyes trained on the ranch house. Behind them, the San Pedro snaked southward, and the mountains to the east were limned in the first rays of sunrise. Alert, their nerves keyed to a fight, they waited for Starbuck's signal.

Still very much in command, Earp was nonetheless relying on Starbuck for advice. Last night, shortly after departing Tombstone, he had summoned Starbuck to the front of the column. On the Charleston road, riding west toward the San Pedro, they had discussed the opening move in their search for Brocius. Starbuck had advanced the argument that a manhunt was not all that different from chasing Indians. Swift strikes, and the element of surprise, were everything to experienced Indian fighters. Their tactics were simple yet deadly effective. Hit fast, hit hard, and strike when least expected. With a poker face, he had then invented several fairy tales about his own days on the owlhoot. Hopping from lie to lie, he told Earp that he had survived only by reversing the tables on lawmen.

His service as an army scout had taught him to deny
them the tactical advantage of surprise.

Earp bought the argument. By midnight, when they
turned north along the San Pedro, he'd begun thinking
of Starbuck as his chief tactician. An hour before
dawn, when they tethered their horses downstream, he
had agreed to Starbuck's plan for storming the Clanton
ranch. Earp stood aside, nodding approval, while Starbuck handed out assignments. Holliday, Vermillion
and McMasters would take the cook shack and the
bunkhouse. Earp and Warren, along with Starbuck
himself, would take the main house. The raid, Starbuck had informed them, would be carried out as
though the entire Brocius gang was bedded down in
the buildings. The likelihood of that was slight, but
he'd warned the men to take no chances. Surprise and
caution were the watchwords.

For his part, Starbuck had all he could do to keep
a straight face. There was virtually no chance that Brocius would be caught napping at the gang's customary
headquarters. The sole purpose of this morning's drill
was to solidify his own position with Earp. That was
essential to the vague plan already taking shape in his
mind. Earp must not only trust him, but must become
dependent on his advice. Then, somewhere down the
line, the opportunity would arise for the wrong word
at the right time. And Earp would go home in a box.

One eye on the ranch house, Starbuck pondered the
thicket of possibilities open to him. The murder warrant, coupled with Earp's decision to remain in Arizona Territory, presented several options. The most
enticing was that Brocius and Earp could be maneu-

vered into a shootout. Stymied until now, it was his original plan and still seemed the most likely to succeed. Failing that, he would attempt to arrange a clash between the Earps and the Behan posse. After last night, he had every confidence the sheriff would be gnashing his teeth for another crack at Earp. Finally, as a last resort, there was the alternative of arresting Earp and delivering him for trial in Tucson. Yet that was the bottom of the barrel, the most chancey of the lot, and Starbuck's expectations were still high. He thought today would put them on the road to the most satisfactory outcome. A permanent sort of good riddance.

Soon after dawn the sun crested the distant mountains. Starbuck waited until the glare of the fireball was at their backs, then he gave the signal. The men scrambled out of the arroyo and rushed across an open stretch of ground. Near the corral, which held fewer than a dozen horses, they separated into two groups. Holliday hurried toward the cook shack, while McMasters and Vermillion burst through the door of the bunkhouse. Starbuck, with Earp and Warren on his heels, stormed into the main house.

Starbuck and Earp quickly checked the three bedrooms at the rear of the house. All were empty, and looked as though no one had slept there in several days. Warren came out of the kitchen as they returned to the front room. He shook his head, indicating he'd found nothing. Walking to a pot-bellied stove, Starbuck bent over and placed his hand on the underside of the firebox. He straightened up, affirmation written across his features.

"Stone cold," he said. "Hasn't been used for at least two days, maybe more."

"You called it," Earp acknowledged. "They probably cleared out the same night they shot Morg."

"Left in a hurry, too." Starbuck gestured at a disarray of clothing and gear scattered about the room. "When they missed you and Doc at the pool hall, that put a crimp in their plans. I'd judge Brocius decided it was time to pull another disappearing act."

"All I want to know——"

"Look here what we found!"

Holliday shoved a bewhiskered little man through the door. He was on the sundown side of forty, nearly bald, and stooped from a lifetime of standing over a cook stove. Barefooted, the trap door of his longjohns hanging loose, he stumbled to a halt. His eyes were wide with fear.

"Almost missed him," Holliday chuckled. "Sherm remembered to check the outhouse, and found him taking a constitutional."

Earp gave him a cool once-over. "You remember me?"

"Guess I do," the cook admitted shakily. "My arm ain't been the same since the last time you stopped by."

"You remember the question I asked you then?"

"Couldn't hardly forget. You asked me where Brocius and the boys had went to."

"I'm askin' you again."

The cook turned pallid as a gravestone. "I shore hate to tell you this, but the answer's the same. I ain't got no more idea than the man in the moon." He shot a weak glance around at the men. "It's the holy-honest-to-Christ's truth! Them boys don't never say boo to me."

"You're not deaf, are you?"

"I do my best," the cook mumbled. "What you don't hear can't hurt you."

"Wanna bet?" Earp motioned to Vermillion and McMasters. "Unplug his ears."

Vermillion, who was standing to the rear, drove his fist into the cook's kidneys. The little man doubled over, his eyes bulging with pain. His mouth popped open in a breathless whoofing sound. McMasters struck out in a fast shadowy movement. His blow connected with a mushy crack, and the cook lurched backwards, spurting blood from a broken nose. McMasters clubbed him upside the ear, then drove a whistling haymaker deep into his rib cage. The cook dropped like a wet bag of sand. He moaned, spitting frothy bubbles, and sucked great gasps of air.

Earp watched the beating with stolid indifference. But when Vermillion cocked his leg for a kick, Starbuck moved to stop it. He stepped in, shielding the cook, and waved Vermillion off.

"That's enough! He's no good to us if he can't talk."

Starbuck knelt down. "Listen to me, old man. I'll only ask once, and you'd better have an answer."

The cook stared up at him, lips puckered like a goldfish. Starbuck gave him a moment, then leaned closer. "Tell me one thing. When Brocius and his boys rode out, which direction were they headed?"

"East," the cook rasped, breathing heavily. "Acrost the river."

Starbuck climbed to his feet. "That's all we need. I checked the ground, and that thunder storm didn't get this far south. It'll be easy tracking."

Vermillion nudged the cook with his toe. "What about him?"

"Kill him," Earp said with chilling simplicity.

"No!" Starbuck turned, meeting Earp's look directly. "You start killing innocent people and we'll have to run all the way to China. I won't be a party to it."

"What's to stop me?"

"Nothing," Starbuck said evenly. "Except you'll have to find yourself another tracker."

"You've gone squeamish awful sudden."

"I've killed my share, but I never murdered anybody. I'd like to keep it that way."

"What the hell!" Earp laughed a strange, cryptic laugh. "Wouldn't want to hurt your sensitive feelings."

He stepped past the cook and walked toward the door. Starbuck, breathing an inward sigh of relief, followed him outside. The others exchanged quizzical glances, then slowly filed along behind.

Some ten minutes later McMasters and Vermillion brought the horses from downstream. Starbuck, watched closely by Earp, was walking the shoreline east of the river. Suddenly he stopped, dropping to one knee, and studied the faint imprint of tracks in the ground. He took a smidge of dirt between his fingers, nodding to himself as though the earth possessed some secret knowledge. Then he rose and walked back to Earp.

"Eight horses." He bobbed his head into a blinding sunrise. "Tracks are three days old."

"You're sure?" Earp regarded him with squinted eyes. "I wouldn't take kindly to a wild-goose-chase."

Starbuck nodded. "I'm sure."

"Then let's ride."

Florentino Cruz reminded himself to light a candle to the Virgin. A swarthy man of mixed blood, he treated religion with the superstition of one who believes that all gods are whimsical and must be constantly appeased. He thought it would be a serious error not to offer thanks for his good fortune.

A bandit, and more recently an assassin, he sometimes took refuge with his sister and her husband. Their small rancho lay on the western slope of the Dragoon Mountains. Some twenty miles northeast of Tombstone, it was off the beaten track, tucked away in a remote stretch of wilderness. Cruz's brother-in-law raised goats and pigs, and tended a vegetable garden he had scratched out of the rocky soil. In a stout log corral, he also kept an unusually large number of horses. A poor man, cursed with a barren wife, he saw no harm in supplementing his meager income. His wife's brother rode with a band of gringos, and their leader treated him with the generosity of a patron. In return, he operated a relay station for the Brocius gang.

Cruz often stopped over here when a job was completed. His sister's cooking was spicy and plentiful, and he much preferred it to the swill served at the

Clanton ranch. Furthermore, he was of the strong opinion that he was safer here. The gang's secret hideout,
in his view, was not secret enough. Only this morning,
following Stilwell's death last night, the gang had ridden off on fresh mounts. He had elected to remain
behind, certain in the knowledge that Brocius would
draw pursuit. He considered it unfortunate, almost an
omen, that Earp had not been killed at the train station.
He also considered himself a wise man for having separated from his gringo *compañeros*. Here, with his sister and her husband, he was out of harm's way.

In the deepening indigo of dusk, Cruz and his
brother-in-law were splitting wood outside the one-
room adobe. His sister appeared in the doorway and
tossed a pan of dirty water into the yard. She wiped
her hands on her dress, and stood for a moment watching the men. Then, on the verge of turning back into
the house, she suddenly stiffened. She stared west,
shielding her eyes against the dying flare of sunset.
Some distance away, she saw three riders top a low
rise. Their features were indistinct, but their clothing
immediately identified them as gringos.

The men, following her gaze, stopped splitting
wood. The riders moved toward them at a slow trot,
silhouetted against the last rays of daylight. Then,
emerging into the silty dusk, their features became visible. Cruz instantly recognized the two Earp brothers,
and the stranger he'd seen with them at the train station. He dropped his ax, jerking a pistol from the
waistband of his trousers. His eyes flicked to the
adobe, then he quickly changed his mind. He ran toward the corral.

As he rounded the corner of the house, Cruz broke stride and skidded to an abrupt halt. Three more riders, one of them Doc Holliday, were circling the corral from the north. Behind him, he heard the thud of hoof-beats as the Earps spurred their horses to a gallop. Trapped and desperate, he sprinted toward a wooded outcropping east of the corral. Before he could reach the knoll, Holliday and the men he recognized as *pistoleros* cut him off. A moment later Earp and his companions closed in from the rear.

Cruz flung his sixgun on the ground and raised his hands. He watched with a doglike dumbfounded stare as the riders joined ranks in a loose, halfmoon formation. No one spoke, but he felt Earp's gaze boring into him with the intensity of fire. The horses advanced, crowding ever closer, and he scuttled backwards to avoid being trampled. Slowly, relentlessly, the riders forced him up the knoll. At the crest, still backing away, he lost his balance and tumbled head over heels down the reverse slope. The horsemen kneed their mounts into the defile and reined to a halt before him. Dazed and shaken, he hauled himself to his feet.

Earp's jaw muscles worked, and his eyes narrowed to tiny points of malevolence. He shifted in his saddle, glancing at Starbuck. A cruel smile touched his lips.

"This here's Florentino Cruz," he said without inflection. "Sometimes known as Indian Charlie."

"Wasn't he one of the men named in the indictment for killing Morg?"

Earp merely nodded, then turned to Vermillion. "Ask him if he knows who I am."

Vermillion leaned forward. *"Conoces este hombre?"*

"Sí, este hombre se llama Earp."

"Tell him"—Earp's voice dropped—"I came here to kill him for what he did to my brother."

Vermillion ducked his chin at Earp. *"Este hombre está aquí para matarte. Por la cosa tu hiciste a su hermano."*

"Madre Dios!" Cruz dropped to his knees, clasping his hands like a man offering prayer. *"Por favor yo soy innocente! Yo no quiero morir!"*

Vermillion spat tobacco juice on the ground. "Says he didn't do it."

"Gutless bastard!" Earp made a quick, savage gesture. "Tell him he's got one chance to live. I'll let him go if he tells us where to find Brocius."

"Díle a ellos donde está Brocius y este hombre no le mata."

Cruz blanched at the mention of Brocius' name. He darted an imploring look at the other men, only to be met by grim stares. After a moment, Earp pulled his sawed-off shotgun from the saddle boot and slowly cocked both hammers. Kneeing his horse to the right, he laid the shotgun over the saddle horn and lowered the muzzle until it was centered on Cruz's head. The halfbreed's eyes went round as saucers. His gaze was riveted on the shotgun, never wavering from the double black holes in the stubby muzzle.

Earp wagged the tip of the shotgun. "Tell him he's got five seconds to talk or he'll be shakin' hands with his maker."

"Usted tiene cinco segundos para hablar o usted va con Jesus Cristo muy pronto."

Cruz swallowed, his voice choked with terror. *"Brocius y siete de los hombres están en Iron Springs."*

"We got it," Vermillion said, easing back in his saddle. "He says Brocius and six or seven of the gang are holed up at Iron Springs. Near as I recollect, that's over in the Whetstone Mountains."

Starbuck, looking on, knew the halfbreed had sealed his own death warrant. But this time he raised no objections. Cruz was a murderer, one of a gang of cutthroats, and he felt not the slightest stirring of mercy. Nor was he at odds with what Earp was about to do. He himself had hung men for lesser crimes, and an execution, whatever the reason, was still an execution. Some men deserved to die.

The shotgun exploded in a double roar. Cruz's head seemed to evaporate. His skull blew apart and he was knocked kicking onto his back. A mist of bone and brain matter rained down, covering his torso with a light, blood-red spray. His legs jerked, bootheels pounding the earth in a slow dance of death. Then, with one last twitch, it stopped.

Earp reined his horse around and rode off. The others trailed him over the knoll and down past the corral. Out front of the adobe, the Mexican and the halfbreed woman were standing with their heads bowed. Earp signaled a halt, and the men reined in their mounts directly behind him. When the dust settled, he broke open the shotgun, ejecting the spent shells, and reloaded. Then he jammed it into the saddle boot, and turned his gaze on the couple. His eyes were cold and impassive, his mouth razored in a tight line. He motioned to Vermillion.

"Tell'em Cruz is dead." He dug out a gold coin and tossed it in the dirt at their feet. "Twenty dollars ought to buy a real impressive mass. Tell'em if they're smart, they'll report he got bit by a scorpion and didn't recover."

Vermillion indicated the coin. *"Su amigo está muerto. Si ustedes son listos reportarán que él fue picado por un escorpión."*

The man removed his sombrero, looking down at the coin, and bobbed his head. The woman stood stockstill, her eyes frozen on the patch of ground at her feet. Earp was silent for a time, seemingly lost in thought. Watching him, Starbuck sensed he was debating the wisdom of leaving them alive. Then, on sudden impulse, he apparently decided the gold piece would buy their silence. He brought his horse sharply around and spurred off into the gathering darkness.

The men kicked their mounts into a lope and rode after him. The thud of hoofbeats slowly diminished, and within moments the riders were lost to sight.

The sister of Florentino Cruz crossed herself and slowly collapsed in the doorway. Her husband stooped down, wiping dust off the coin, and stuck it in his pocket. He went inside the adobe, returning a moment later with a lighted lantern and a shovel. He walked in the direction of the knoll.

CHAPTER 16

"Foxy bastard!"

"Who's that?"

"Brocius," Earp said roughly. "You had him pegged all along."

"Only about halfway."

"C'mon, Jack, credit due where credit's deserved! You said he had a hideout somewhere close to home, and you hit the mark dead center. Iron Springs couldn't be no more than ten or twelve miles from the Clanton place."

"Maybe so," Starbuck said doubtfully. "Only he's lots trickier than I thought."

"So he doubled back! How the hell could you've figured that?"

"He didn't double back."

Earp gave him a swift sidelong look. "What are you gettin' at?"

"Well, I've been studying on it. Something kept me scratching my head, but it didn't rightly make sense."

"I thought you was awful quiet last night."

"Tell you the truth, it only come to me a little while ago."

The statement was a baldfaced lie. Last night, after the Cruz killing, they had camped on a small creek some miles to the west. There, following a cold supper, Starbuck had reconstructed the events of the past three days. Bit by bit, based on what he'd learned, he pieced together the movements of the Brocius gang since the night of Morg's death. Yet he'd held his silence last night, retiring early to his blankets. All day today, as they rode westerly toward the Whetstone Mountains, he had also avoided conversation with Earp. Somehow, turning it this way and that, he had searched for a means of twisting the situation to Earp's disadvantage. But now, lacking any great brainstorm, he saw nothing to lose by playing it straight. Earp would be impressed and come to rely even more heavily on his advice. Which at some point would prove vital to his overall plan.

"Yesterday morning," Starbuck said at length, "when I found the tracks at Clanton's place. You remember I said they were three days old?"

"What about it?"

"That should've tipped me off. Those tracks were made the night Morg was killed."

"So?"

"Well, the way I put it together, Brocius and his bunch swapped horses at Cruz's place the next morning. Then they rode straight to Tucson, and tried to waylay us at the train station. Afterward, they turned right around and rode back to Cruz's place."

"And swapped horses again!" Earp suddenly grasped it. "That means they were headed west toward Iron Springs at the same time we were followin' their tracks east to the Dragoons."

"We're a day late and a dollar short," Starbuck affirmed. "Lucky for us, Cruz decided to stay behind. Otherwise, I would've had to start tracking all over again. No telling how much time we would've lost."

Earp uttered a low chuckle. "I'd sooner be a day late and a dollar short than no payday at all. That's what happened the last time I took out after Brocius."

Starbuck cracked a smile. "All you needed was a hound dog. Brocius lays so many trails, it takes a damn good sniffer to pick up the scent."

"Jack, you're all right!" Earp said, with a quick nod of satisfaction. "You can scout for me six days a week and all day on Sunday. Hadn't been for you, we'd still be wonderin' which way was up."

Starbuck gave himself a pat on the back. Once more he'd euchred Earp into accepting a highly embroidered version of the facts. As the sun rose to its zenith, and they forded the San Pedro north of Contention, he felt like a cat with a mouthful of feathers. He had a hunch today was the day. The end of the line.

The sun sank lower, smothering in a bed of copper beyond the mountains. The ragged crests jutted skyward like sentinels guarding a cruel and lifeless land. Far below, bordered by a grove of trees, the springs lay hidden in purple shadow. There was no sound, only the foreboding silence of oncoming night.

The men reined to a halt on a craggy ridge over-

looking the springs. A narrow trail led downward
to the wooded gorge, winding around a rocky spur
near the bottom. Starbuck dismounted, quickly inspecting the trail where it sloped steeply off the ridge.
He grunted to himself, spotting marks left by shod
horses in the hard-packed ground. After closer exam-
ination, he turned and indicated the tracks with a
sweeping motion of his arm.

Earp told the other men to stay with the horses. He
walked forward and joined Starbuck at the edge of the
escarpment. They went belly down, removing their
hats, and began a systematic inspection of the basin
below. The springs was plainly visible, a cool waterhole freshened from deep within the earth's core. The
shelterbelt of trees, thick with undergrowth and obscured by shadow, curved in a gentle arc beyond the
springs. There was no movement, no picket line of
horses, no sign of man. To all appearances, only wilderness creatures came to drink at Iron Springs.

Earp looked perplexed. "What the hell do you make
of that?"

"Beats me," Starbuck said, studying the springs intently. "Looks dead as a doornail down there."

"No way they could've known we're on their trail."

"You reckon they're camped back in those trees?"

"I dunno," Earp confessed. "If they are, why don't
we see smoke from a fire? They'd have no reason to
pitch a cold camp."

"Well, I know one thing," Starbuck said with conviction. "Those tracks were made yesterday. Somebody went down that trail before nightfall."

"Then where the Jesus are they?"

"Is there another way out of here?"

"Could be," Earp allowed, pointing south along the gorge. "The ground seems to drop off in that direction. Maybe something spooked them and they've done hightailed it."

"I guess there's only one way to find out."

"What's that?"

"Somebody has to go down there and have a look-see."

Earp glanced sidewise. "You volunteerin' for the job?"

"Got no choice." Starbuck grinned shallowly. "I'm the dumbbell that signed on as scout with this outfit."

"All right, but you take it slow and easy. We'll cover you from up here just in case things aren't as peaceful as they look. Any sign of trouble, you hump your butt out of there muy damn pronto."

"Don't worry! I'm a regular streak of lightning when I put my mind to it."

Starbuck was playing a longshot. He recalled the last words out of Florentino Cruz's mouth, and he couldn't believe the halfbreed had lied. He thought there was at least a fifty-fifty chance that Brocius had posted a lookout here on the ridge. If true, that meant the gang had been alerted, and was now waiting in the copse of trees below. Somehow, without getting himself killed, he had to lure Earp down to the springs. He was betting that Brocius wouldn't betray his position merely to kill one man. He took cold comfort from the thought that Brocius had only one known obsession, Wyatt Earp. He hoped, at last, to bring them together.

Without a word to the others, he went back to his horse and mounted. As he rode down the trail, he saw Earp positioning them along the rim of the cliff. Then he turned his attention to the dusky basin. Daylight was fading rapidly, and he knew he hadn't a moment to spare. Even Brocius and his bushwhackers needed enough light to see their sights.

At the bottom of the trail, he rode straight toward the springs. Holding his horse to a steady walk, he circled the waterhole and reined to a halt on the far side. He was within ten yards of the treeline, and a perfect target. He twisted around in the saddle, slowly scanning the shadowed thickets. He saw nothing and heard nothing. Yet an odd shiver went up his back-bone, as though he'd caught a whisper of wind whistling through the eyesockets of a skull. His instinct, strong enough to set his skin tingling, told him they were there. He knew they were watching him, trigger fingers tensed and ready, waiting for him to sound the alarm. He let his eyes rove through the trees a moment longer, then he kneed his horse into a walk. All the way around the springs, the hair on the back of his neck was stiff as broomstraw. He told himself with mute wonder that he'd been a damn fool. But he sensed he had won the gamble. There would be no shots. Not yet.

His horse took the steep grade in a series of bounding lurches. Once more on top, he stepped from the saddle and calmly lit a cheroot. His guts were quivering, but he struck and doused the match with a steady hand.

"Well talk up!" Earp demanded, hurrying forward. "What'd you see?"

"Quiet as a church," Starbuck said, exhaling smoke. "I think you hit the nail on the head. Brocius and his boys must've spooked and took off for parts unknown."

The other men collected around Earp, their faces expectant and sober. A moment slipped past, then Holliday let go a muttered curse. He regarded Starbuck with narrow suspicion.

"I don't like it! Something don't smell right."

"Tell you what, Doc." Starbuck inspected the tip of his cigar. "If you're not satisfied, why don't you ride on down there and check it out for yourself?"

"No need." Earp waved them apart. "I'm satisfied, and that's all that counts. We'll just have to pick up their trail come first light and see where it leads."

"What about tonight?" Holliday persisted. "I don't much like the idea of campin' at the springs."

"Quit borrowin' trouble," Earp admonished him. "Nobody shot Jack! Besides, the horses need water, and we could all use a decent night's sleep. Let's get mounted."

In the deepening twilight, the men gathered their horses. Earp led the way, followed by Holliday and Warren. Starbuck managed to position himself in the center, with Vermillion and McMasters bringing up the rear. They went down the narrow trail single-file, the jangle of saddle gear chiming musically in the stillness. No one spoke, and Starbuck took that as a good sign. The men were weary, their senses dulled after nearly four days in the saddle. Except for Holliday,

none of them had shown any concern about camping
at the springs. They had come here prepared for a
fight, and there was a natural letdown upon learning
that Brocius had once again eluded their grasp. Starbuck thought it was near-perfect, their mood tailor-
made for an ambush. His single qualm was not for his
own safety, but rather that one of the outlaws would
suddenly turn trigger-happy. Timing was essential, and
he worried that the trap might yet be spoiled.

The trail bottomed out and Earp reined toward the
springs. One by one, the men rode forward, loosely
grouped behind him. The gorge was rapidly turning
dark, and ahead, the grove of trees was cloaked in inky
shadow. Then, like blinking fireflies, a row of guns
spat flame all along the treeline.

Earp's saddle horn disintegrated and his hat flew
off his head. He kicked free of the stirrups, grabbing
his shotgun, and dove headlong from the saddle. He
landed on his side and rolled over, thumbing back the
hammer as he came to rest on his stomach. Across the
waterhole, the trees were now alive with the fiery blast
of gunshots. He slammed the scattergun into his shoulder and centered on a muzzle flash. When he pulled
the trigger, a man screamed and stumbled out of the
underbrush. He fired the second barrel and saw the
man go down. Then he tossed the shotgun aside and
jerked his pistol.

Behind him, the men had quit their horses and hit
the ground. With the exception of Warren's horse,
they had survived the first volley unscathed. Veterans
of countless shootouts, they reacted almost instinc-
tively after the initial shock of the ambush. The gunfire

became general as they quickly joined the fight. Bellied down, they made poor targets despite the storm of lead whistling across the waterhole. The crack of the outlaws' rifles was punctuated by the dull boom of their own sixguns. Unlike the outlaws, however, they were not scattering their shots in a random barrage. Instead, making each bullet count, they fixed on a muzzle flash and aimed slightly to the right. Accuracy under darkened conditions was difficult, but their fire had a telling effect. A howl indicated that at least one of the gang had been wounded, and another fell thrashing at the edge of the treeline. Yet the fight quickened in tempo, and the sound of gunfire rose to a staccato roar. A patchwork of snarling lead hissed back and forth across the springs.

From his position in the center, Starbuck hugged the ground and poured a steady fire into the trees. He was aware of Warren, who was shooting from behind the fallen horse, and he heard the bark of guns off to one side. But he was too busy to count, and he had no idea who might have been wounded or killed. When he emptied the Colt, he rolled to a new position and reloaded all six chambers. His next shot drew return fire, two quick rounds. One slug kicked dirt in his face and the other fried the air around his ears. Beside a tree, momentarily revealed in the muzzle flash, he saw the bare outlines of a man's face. He dropped his sights a notch and thumbed off three shots, rapid fire. Almost instantly there was a downward flash as the rifle fired into the ground, and the man pitched sideways into the undergrowth. Then, too suddenly to comprehend, all firing from the treeline abruptly ceased.

Several more shots were fired by the Earp party before they realized the fight was over. A stillness settled across the spring, and moments later the rumble of hooves filtered through the trees. A blur of horses, almost invisible in the darkness, suddenly bolted from the far end of the grove. The riders whipped their mounts into a gallop and were quickly gone, clattering south through the gorge. Within seconds, even the thud of hoofbeats faded to nothing.

Starbuck stood, holstering his gun, and went slack-jawed. He saw Earp not twenty feet in front of him, and for an instant, he couldn't credit his own eyes. He recalled hearing the shotgun, but he'd assumed that Earp, who was in the vanguard, had taken the brunt of the gang's fire. Now, stunned speechless, a sullen coal of rage exploded in his chest. All the conniving and trickery had come to nothing. The ambush, endangering his own life to force a showdown, all for nothing. Earp, seemingly immune to death, had emerged without a scratch.

His fists balled into hard knots, and he uttered a low brutish curse.

Starbuck's sense of outrage and disgust was quickly compounded. Earp ordered a fire built, and it soon became clear that Warren's horse was the only casualty. Holliday had been grazed along the cheekbone, and Vermillion had suffered a flesh wound, but the others were untouched. By the light of the fire, it was also apparent that Earp enjoyed a state of grace almost beyond belief. His clothes hung in tatters. There were three holes through his coat, another drilled through his hat, and a slug was imbedded in the heel of his boot. Not one had drawn blood.

Starbuck's anger slowly gave way to bemused wonderment. Never a staunch believer, he nonetheless asked himself what god it was that watched over these men. Or perhaps it wasn't a god at all. Perhaps there was some special devil, a satanic force that protected such men from harm. Certainly no five men had ever had a closer brush with death. Within the space of three or four minutes, these men had been on the receiving end of probably a hundred rifle slugs. Yet none of them had been killed, and the wounds they'd suffered were hardly worse than the nick of a dull razor. It defied understanding, and a thought occurred that left him momentarily chilled. Perhaps, after all, Wyatt Earp wasn't meant to be killed. Perhaps he was *unkillable*.

The idea was foreign to Starbuck's character. No man, himself included, led a charmed life. Nor was there any great mystery that he too had come through tonight unscathed. There was a time and place for every man to die, and when a man's number was called, he answered. Earp wasn't unkillable. Tonight simply hadn't been his night. Starbuck vowed to himself he would cancel that reprieve, at the right time and the right place. However long it took.

In the light of the fire, it was revealed that three outlaws had answered the call. One of them was the man Starbuck had shot, three neat holes stitched beneath his breastbone. Another, whose identity was un-

known, had been dusted front and back by several
pistol slugs. The third man, however, was instantly
recognizable. Curly Bill Brocius had taken a double
load of buckshot directly above his beltbuckle. His
shirtfront was a plate-sized starburst of blood and gore.
He was eviscerated, quite literally blown to bits.

Earp seemed to derive no satisfaction from the outlaw leader's death. There was no question his shotgun
had done the job, but his expression betrayed no hint
of vindication. Staring down at the body, he appeared
curiously disgruntled, somehow unappeased. After a
long while, he looked up, his features set in a tight
scowl. His gaze settled on McMasters.

"Sherm, get a rope."

"A rope?"

"String him up in the tallest tree you can find."

McMasters looked startled. "You mean hang him?"

"That's exactly what I mean."

"Why hell, Wyatt, he's already dead."

"Do it!" Earp commanded. "Before the buzzards
pick his bones, I want every backshooter in the territory to get the message. So hang him high."

Starbuck watched the hanging with a sense of the
unreal. McMasters and Vermillion dragged the body
under a tree and tossed the rope over a stout limb.
Then they hoisted the body high in the air and snubbed
the rope tight around the base of the tree. The job
finished, they walked away as though they had taken
part in something unnormal, not altogether human.
The dead man overhead seemed to mock them all.

Earp turned and walked to the fire. He held out his

hands to the flames, and a sudden tremor rippled along his jawbone. Looking on, Starbuck was reminded of a man he'd seen in a courtroom long ago. A man on his way to the madhouse.

CHAPTER 17

In the darkness, the campfire was a small island of light. The men, after wolfing down their supper, were seated on the ground. No one spoke, and the cheery blaze did nothing to dispel a sense of gloom.

Vermillion and McMasters, assigned the first guard shift, were posted along the south end of the grove. Holliday, immediately after the hanging, had insisted on mounting a watch. None of them believed the gang would return, but they all felt more comfortable with someone standing guard. Their horses, picketed at the edge of the treeline, were also kept near at hand. Standing hipshot and drowsy, the animals were visible in the flickering glow of the fire.

Over the crackle of flames, the only sound was the measured creak of a rope. The body, little more than a dim shape in the erratic light, was pushed gently to and fro by an evening breeze. Earp, who hadn't spoken in the last hour, stared at the hanged man with a vacant expression. His eyes had a faraway look, as if he was gazing at something obscured by distance. He sat perfectly still, legs crossed and hands dangling over his knees. The sawed-off shotgun was cradled in his lap.

The long, stony silence was at last broken by Holliday. His tone was caustic, laced with hostility. His remark was addressed directly to Starbuck.

"You're one piss-poor scout, Johnson."

Starbuck was hard put to suppress a smile, but he managed an offhand answer. "All's well that ends well."

"Like hell!" Holliday said furiously. "You come pretty goddamn close to gettin' us killed."

"Easy to say when you've got hindsight on your side."

After the fight, Holliday had taken a torch and walked off into the trees. Halfway through the grove, he'd found a camp site, the fire hastily extinguished and still smoldering. On the far side of the wooded thicket, he had stumbled upon a picket line, with the horses of the three dead outlaws standing walleyed in the night. Since then, he had kept to himself, sullen and withdrawn. Now, in a burst of temper, his anger spilled out.

"Hindsight's got nothin' to do with it! Anybody with a lick of sense would've spotted something fishy. You'd have to be blind to miss it!"

"The way it worked out," Starbuck said lightly, "there wasn't anything to miss. Brocius must've had a lookout posted up there on the ridge. He had plenty of warning, all the time he needed."

"Don't change the subject," Holliday grated. "We're talkin' about you, not Brocius."

"What I'm saying," Starbuck explained, "is that

Brocius probably had a good half hour to make his move. He could've cut and run long before we got here. Instead, he used that time to fix up a real fine ambush."

"That's right!" Warren put in. "You saw it your ownself, Doc. The way they'd doused the fire, and had their horses picketed on the back side of the trees. Brocius was cagey as hell! He rigged a trap and just waited for us to ride into it."

"And we did!" Holliday said sharply. "With Johnson's help, it worked slick as a whistle."

"Help?" Starbuck looked offended. "You're off your rocker, Doc! It was me that rode down here and took a chance on getting ventilated. Or maybe you forgot that?"

"You'd like me to forget, wouldn't you?"

"What the devil's that supposed to mean?"

"You led us in here like a goddamn Judas goat and got us drygulched. That's what it means—plain and simple."

"Doc, you've got a mighty short memory."

"Oh yeah?" Holliday bridled. "What'd I forget now?"

"Couple of things," Starbuck said lazily. "Just for openers, I was getting shot at, too. So it's not like you were all by your lonesome. On top of that, out of the three we killed, I cooled one of them myself. If you care to count the holes, they're dead center through the brisket. All in all, I'd say I carried my share of the load and then some."

"Damn good thing," Holliday grumbled sourly. "If you hadn't, I would've put out your lights myself."

"C'mon, Doc!" Warren laughed uneasily. "Christ, nobody's perfect. Brocius and his boys were hid so well anybody could've missed spottin' them. Isn't that right, Jack?"

"Well—" Starbuck gave him a jolly wink. "Doc might've tumbled to them, but then we'll never know, will we? He seemed real happy to stay up on the ridge and let me come down here for a looksee."

Holliday skewered him with a glare. "You've already pushed your luck enough for one night."

"Who, me?" Starbuck opened his hands, shrugged. "I was just funning you, Doc. No harm in that."

"You're liable to fun yourself—"

"Quit your squabblin'!"

Earp's voice brought them around. His spell appeared broken, and it seemed some cord of sanity had kept him from slipping over the edge. His face was drawn and solemn, and his tone was irritable.

"You want to fight amongst yourselves, save it till another time. We've got plans to make."

Holliday was watching him carefully. "What sort of plans?"

"Johnny Ringo."

"What about him?"

"I'll tell you what about him," Earp said harshly. "He's the only one that ever saw us together. We've got to run him down."

"Be a waste of time," Holliday observed. "I know that bunch. None of them could hardly take a leak without instructions from Brocius. With him dead, they'll scatter all over hell and half of Mexico."

"You're not listenin'," Earp said with strained patience. "Until Ringo's dead and buried, I'll always be lookin' over my shoulder. He's the only one that knows—*the only one!*"

"Give it up, Wyatt." Holliday's tone softened, turned persuasive. "It's time we started worryin' about murder, not robbery. The way things stand, Ringo's the least of our troubles."

Starbuck felt a jolt of excitement. The link he'd sought all these months had just been revealed. He had no idea of the circumstances involved, no hint as to when it had occurred. Yet there was no question as to its meaning. Johnny Ringo could tie Earp to the stage robberies!

"Doc's right." Warren placed a hand on his brother's shoulder, reassuring him. "We've evened the score for Morg, but we can't afford to stay in the territory much longer. If we try chasin' Ringo down, it's us that's liable to get caught. And you'd never get off, not for murder."

"Frank Stilwell," Earp said quietly, "was a good-for-nothin' backshooter. Him and Cruz both deserved to die."

"Maybe they did," Holliday agreed. "But that don't change the shape of things. Behan's on our trail, and sooner or later, he's bound to get us cornered. Once he does, he'll move heaven and earth to put us on the gallows. You know it for a fact, too."

"So you're sayin' we should run, is that it?"

Holliday nodded. "We've played out our string. No sense bettin' into a cold deck when there's always a new game somewhere else."

"I suppose," Earp said in a resigned voice. "You got any place special in mind?"

"Colorado," Holliday replied quickly. "Behan wouldn't never figure us to head north. That's why we haven't run across him up till now. He's probably got the whole Mexican border covered like a mustard plaster."

A tight fist of apprehension suddenly gripped Starbuck. With Earp in Arizona, there were several options open to him. At least two murder charges were outstanding, which made every lawman in the territory Starbuck's ally. There was, moreover, the new possibility presented by Johnny Ringo. He had no idea where it would lead, or even how it might be turned to advantage. Yet it would be of no advantage whatever in Colorado. He had the sinking feeling that everything was suddenly falling apart.

"Doc's on the right track," Warren said earnestly. "Once we're across the line into Colorado, they couldn't touch us in a month of Sundays. It'd be a whole new ball of wax. A fresh start!"

"A fresh start." Earp's voice was abstracted. "How many times would that make?"

"How many times what?"

"Three, four," Earp mumbled to himself. "We've started over so many times I've lost count."

"One thing about it," Holliday said morosely. "It beats the hell out of having your neck stretched."

Earp inclined his head in a faint nod. "No argument there. I just don't like the idea of leavin' loose ends."

"You talkin' about Ringo?"

"He's about the only loose end left."

"You think about a hangin' rope," Holliday advised him. "That'll take your mind off Ringo."

Earp's gaze drifted to the body swaying overhead. He permitted himself a single ironic glance, and his eyes shuttled away. He turned slowly to look at Holliday.

"We'll pull out at sunrise."

Starbuck felt like he'd been punched in the mouth. All his plans were out the window, and there seemed no alternative to tagging along. His thoughts turned north, to Colorado. He considered a last desperate gamble, a way to end it. Perhaps the only way.

A week later the Earp party rode into Trinidad. They were bone-weary, with the look of men who had ridden hard and traveled light. At one of the town's sleazier hotels, rooms were engaged for the night. There, with plans to meet for breakfast, they separated. Tomorrow seemed time enough to discuss the future.

In his room, Starbuck stripped and poured a pitcher of water into the washbasin. He took a bird-bath, sponging away layers of grime, then used the dirty water to shave. From his saddlebags, he laid out a fresh shirt and a clean pair of trousers. Padding around the room in his undershorts, he lit a cheroot and turned down the bed covers. The bath had refreshed him, but he was hollow-eyed with fatigue and needed sleep. He stretched out on the bed, placing a stone ashtray on his stomach. He blew a slow, thoughtful smoke ring at the ceiling.

Trinidad, he told himself, was a shrewd choice on Earp's part. By rail, it lay some two hundred miles south of Denver. Of greater significance, from a strategic standpoint, it was perfectly situated for a man on the run. Only ten or twelve miles south of town, at the state boundary, Raton Pass provided a gateway into the wilds of northern New Mexico. To the east, perhaps a day's ride away, was No Man's Land, a lawless sanctuary for outlaws and killers. To the southeast, bordering New Mexico and No Man's Land, was the Texas Panhandle, equally remote and bereft of peace officers. Within that unholy trinity, a man could lose himself forever. In the event Earp had to run, there was no better jumping off point than Trinidad. But then, having escaped Arizona, why would it be necessary to run?

The question summoned a thought from some dark corner of Starbuck's mind. For the past few days he'd been toying with a new, and not altogether improbable, idea. The details were still fuzzy, and it was another in a string of longshots he had played so unsuccessfully over the past four months. Yet it was entirely legal, and unlike killing Earp outright, it would boost his stock as a detective. Not that he flinched from killing, but he'd undertaken the assignment with the thought of adding a feather to his cap rather than a notch on his gun. All the same, the critical factor was Earp himself.

Nothing had been said openly, but Starbuck sensed that Trinidad was the end of the line. Tomorrow, Earp would cut the cord and send his band of gunmen their separate ways. Their usefulness to him had ended the day he fled Arizona. Like ragtag soldiers, recruited for the duration of hostilities, they had served their pur-

pose. The war was lost, the last battle fought, and tomorrow they would be mustered out. Their leader,
simply put, no longer needed them.

Vermillion and McMasters doubtless expected to be
sent packing. They were, after all, professionals who
formed alliances rather than personal bonds. As for
Holliday, Starbuck suspected he was in for a surprise,
perhaps the shock of his life. He was about to discover
that all men are expendable. Loyalty was a fragile cur-
rency, and even those who risk death in the name of
friendship ultimately outlive their usefulness. Holliday, so long an asset, had now become a liability. He
was a notorious gunman and certain to attract attention
wherever he might go. All of which meant his time
had come and gone. The man he'd faithfully served
now sought obscurity, not headlines.

Starbuck's decision, then, boiled down to a single
element. If Earp stayed put, then legal means might
yet deliver him into the hands of the hangman. If he
tried to run, assuming a new identity, then he would
have to be killed swiftly, using whatever pretext presented itself. Tomorrow would tell the tale.

Starbuck stubbed out his cheroot and set the ashtray
on the floor. He turned down the lamp, easing back
on the pillow, and closed his eyes. He was asleep almost instantly.

After a late breakfast, Earp led the men to a saloon
across from the hotel. The noontime rush was still an
hour away, and the place was empty except for a few
loafers. He signaled the barkeep, and walked toward
a table at the rear of the room.

Over breakfast, Starbuck had detected traces of the man he'd first met in Tombstone. Apparently a night's sleep had restored Earp's vitality. Of greater consequence, the relative haven of Colorado had quite clearly restored his spirits. He exuded confidence, once more in command of himself and events. The thin cord of sanity was on the mend.

The barkeep brought a bottle and glasses. Earp poured for himself, then passed the bottle around the table. When everyone had a drink, he raised his glass in salute.

"You're as good a bunch as a man ever rode with. Here's mud in your eye!"

The men nodded, pleased by the compliment, and drained their glasses. The bottle once more circled the table, but this time there was no toast. Everyone sensed Earp had something on his mind, and they dutifully waited for him to speak. He took a slow sip of whiskey and set his glass on the table. Then his eyes moved from face to face. He smiled.

"Well, boys, I guess it's time for adios and goodbye. Like the man said, all good things come to an end."

Vermillion bobbed his head agreeably. "Where to from here, Wyatt? Any ideas?"

"Now that you mention it," Earp said briskly, "I was talkin' with the desk clerk before you boys came down this morning. He tells me they've struck it big over at Gunnison."

"Gunnison?" Vermillion repeated blankly. "Never heard of it."

"New silver camp," Earp informed them. "Hundred

miles or so west of Colorado Springs. Way it sounds, it'll make Tombstone look like small potatoes."

McMasters chuckled. "You sound like you got the itch again. Figure Gunnison needs a head dog, do you?"

"Aim high, that's my motto! Nobody ever caught the brass ring with his eyes on the ground."

"Damned if that ain't the truth."

"How about you, Sherm?" Earp inquired. "Headed back to Nogales?"

"Not right off," McMasters said vaguely. "Thought I'd take a little sashay down through Texas."

"Don't say?" Earp glanced at Vermillion. "You boys aren't breakin' up the team, are you?"

Vermillion grinned. "I reckon we'll stick together. Folks always figure they're gettin' two for the price of one."

Earp sipped, quiet a moment. Then his gaze swung to Holliday. "How about you, Doc?"

Holliday looked startled. "What d'you mean?"

"Where're you headed? I'd ask you to come along with me and Warren, but Gunnison's just startin' up. Wouldn't be enough action to suit your style."

There was a long silence. Holliday eyed him with a steady, uncompromising stare. No one, least of all Holliday, had missed the point. Dodge City and Tombstone, all the years in between, were of another time. The slate had been wiped clean, and this time he wasn't being invited along. At length, collecting himself, he gave Earp an ashen grin.

"It's Denver for me," he said casually. "I've got a

taste for bright lights and easy livin'. Tombstone pretty well cured me of mining camps."

"Know what you mean," Earp remarked with false cordiality. "Course, you're always welcome, Doc. Anytime you get the urge, why pop on over and see us." He paused, glancing at Starbuck without much interest. "What about yourself, Jack?"

Starbuck made a spur of the moment decision. His gut-instinct told him Earp was actually headed for Gunnison. That allowed a little leeway in his own plans. A trip to Denver, and a conference with the Wells, Fargo superintendent, suddenly seemed very much in order.

"I'll tag along with Doc," he said in high good humor. "Bright lights and fancy sportin' houses sound awful tempting right about now."

"Christ!" Holliday muttered aloud. "Don't get any fool notions. I play a lone hand, no partners!"

"Wouldn't have you anyway," Starbuck ribbed him. "You're too honest for a grifter like me. Strictly along for the ride, Doc! Good company makes the time fly."

"You just remember that when we get to Denver."

"Say now!" Starbuck said abruptly, turning to Earp. "Just thought of something. When you bring the women up from Tucson, be sure and tell Alice good-bye for me. It's not likely I'll get over Gunnison way."

"I'll do it," Earp said a little too hastily. "She'll be sorry she missed you."

Starbuck heard the lie in his voice. Suddenly it was all the more important that he get to Denver. There were things to be done, and no time to spare. With a broad smile, he raised his glass and looked around the table.

"Here's to you, gents! Better days ahead!"

CHAPTER 18

Alice's hair was loose and unbound. She was still wearing her nightgown and her expression was dreamy. Sitting up in the bed, her legs were drawn up and her chin rested on her knees. She was watching Starbuck dress.

His morning ritual seldom varied. By now, she could anticipate every move, step by step. A short, vigorous scrubbing of teeth and a quick splash in the washbasin. A methodical shave, the razor gliding along his jaw bone with deliberate strokes, followed by a few haphazard rakes of a comb through the sandy thatch of hair. Then he selected one of two suits hanging in the wardrobe and began dressing. His final act, which seemed to require the utmost concentration, was knotting his four-in-hand tie. He stood now before the mirror, adjusting the tie with one last tug.

Today, though, her thoughts were not on the morning ritual. Her eyes followed his every movement but her mind was fastened upon the man himself. She marveled that she could love him so completely. With utter candor, she also considered the fact that he did not love her.

A month ago, at the boardinghouse in Tucson, she had received a wire. His request was simple and straightforward: he asked that she and Mattie join him in Denver. He alluded as well to the fact that they were now on their own and had no compelling reason to remain in Tucson. By then, of course, they knew Earp had departed Arizona one jump ahead of a murder warrant. His exact whereabouts were unknown, and since dumping them at the boardinghouse, he had never once attempted to communicate with Mattie. The conclusion, after all those weeks of silence, was inescapable. They could wait until doomsday and there would be no letter, no message of any kind. He had deserted Mattie.

Jack Johnson's wire had seemed a godsend. They were without funds and without prospects. A woman stranded in Tucson and seeking a livelihood was faced with hard times. Her choices were limited to laundress, cafe waitress, or dancehall girl. Or in the extremity, she could join the girls on crib row, selling herself for whatever the traffic would bear. Alice, her heart thumping wildly, chose instead to join Jack Johnson.

All her arguments directed to Mattie were to no avail. Despondent, drinking heavily, Mattie would listen to no slander aimed at her husband. While she wallowed in self-pity, she still loved him and she was almost irrational in her belief that he would one day send for her. After a night of fruitless wrangling, Alice realized it was hopeless. She could stay, knowing full well Mattie was destined for crib row, or she could take a chance on happiness. She wired Jack Johnson to meet her train in Denver.

There, after a warm and passionate reunion, she learned the truth. With shock and dismay, she sat round-eyed while Jack Johnson slowly revealed himself as Luke Starbuck. He told her the whole story, omitting nothing. He made no excuses, openly admitting that he had used her to cultivate Earp's trust. He went on to explain he'd planned to use her as a witness with regard to Earp's involvement in the Tombstone stage robberies. Holding nothing back, he then related he was working secretly to have Earp and Holliday extradited to Arizona on murder charges. In the event that scheme was successful, her testimony would still prove invaluable. She could corroborate, through personal knowledge, a conspiracy that had ultimately led to cold-blooded murder. At the same time, she could avenge her sister, who was no less a victim of Earp's brutality. At last, looking her straight in the eye, Starbuck had told her of his own feelings. He made no promises, but he clearly cared for her and he was deeply concerned with her welfare. She was free to go or stay as she chose. He hoped she would stay.

She stayed. Nothing he'd told her had changed the way she felt toward him. She was there because he wanted her there. He could just as easily have left her in Tucson and called her to testify at the appropriate time. His interest in her, though he dwelled on her importance to the investigation, was clearly personal. She believed that the night he'd taken her into his confidence, and she still believed it. A month with the man she now knew as Luke Starbuck had only served to heighten her emotional attachment.

Underneath the hard exterior, she had discovered that he was not only gentle but delighted in spoiling her. Their suite in the Brown Palace was small but well appointed, far more luxurious than anything she'd ever known. He insisted on outfitting her in stylish gowns, took her to the theater and the finest restaurants, and lavished her with thoughtful gifts. Even more revealing, he was an attentive lover and seemed never to tire of their madcap romps in bed. She had only one complaint. He was still operating under his alias, and the hotel staff always addressed her as Mrs. Johnson. She would have much preferred Mrs. Starbuck.

Yet marriage, under any name, was a remote possibility. She daydreamed a great deal, but she never deceived herself. For all his gentleness and concern, she understood that the man who shared her bed was wary of any permanent bond. He was drawn by wanderlust and his lodestone was some inner vision of distant places he'd not yet seen. She thought there was little likelihood he would ever marry her. She contented herself with the man and the moment, asking nothing more. It was enough for now, perhaps forever. A treasured time of joy and immense happiness.

Starbuck turned from the mirror, smiling. "How do I look?"

"Very spiffy," she said pertly. "What's the occasion?"

"Today's the day we put Holliday on ice."

Her voice went husky and something odd happened to her face. "Will there be trouble?"

"Let's hope so!" he said with great relish. "I'd welcome the chance to put Holliday away for keeps."

"You—" She hesitated, looking at him seriously. "You'll be careful, won't you?"

He made a small gesture of dismissal. "It's in the bag! You get yourself gussied up and we'll go out on the town tonight."

She smiled uncertainly. "I'll be ready."

"Why don't you write Mattie another letter? Tell her Holliday's in the cooler and her no-account husband is next on the list. Maybe that'll bring her around."

"It's no use," she admitted unhappily. "Mattie won't change. She'll destroy herself before she would betray him."

"Damn shame." He met her eyes, but the words came hard. "She's too good a woman to waste herself in the cribs. Wish she'd listen to reason."

Her lips trembled. "I'm worried about you, not Mattie. It frightens me . . . what you're doing . . . all of it."

"Hey, none of that!"

He walked to the bed and took her chin in his hand. He kissed her softly on the mouth, looked deep into her eyes. "Come on, now, no tears allowed! Let me see a smile."

"Yes, sir." She smiled a sad clown smile. "But don't you dare give him an even break."

"That's the ticket!"

He grinned and quickly crossed the room. At the door, he jammed his hat on his head and gave her a reassuring wink. After he'd gone, she sat for a long while with her hands folded in her lap. Her eyes were veined with fear.

Outside the hotel Starbuck turned onto Larimer Street. It was a sunny morning with a hint of spring in the air. The fine weather made his mood all the more chipper, and he stepped along at a brisk pace. He was whistling softly under his breath.

The long wait, like Denver's prolonged winter storms, had at last drawn to a close. Six weeks ago, upon arriving from Trinidad, he had parted with Holliday at the train station. Since then, though they had seen each other only rarely, he had managed to keep tabs on the lean gambler. The Wells, Fargo agent at Gunnison, sworn to secrecy, also kept him posted on Earp. Time had vindicated his hunch, and it soon became apparent he had no reason for concern. True to form, Earp had designs on Gunnison. He was operating a faro game and slowly forming political alliances.

Starbuck, meanwhile, had set the wheels in motion on his latest plan. Arizona authorities were informed of Earp's whereabouts, and it was suggested that Colorado would act favorably on extradition papers. The plan was well received, but very quickly developed into a political tug-of-war. Sheriff John Behan of Tombstone and Sheriff Bob Paul of Tucson were both determined to be the man who returned Wyatt Earp to Arizona. The battlelines were drawn at the territorial capital, and shortly degenerated into a stalemate. The credit for capturing Earp seemed somehow more important than the act itself.

Only last night word had arrived that a solution was near at hand. The details were as yet unknown, but Starbuck took it as a positive sign. Working with Wells, Fargo, he had concocted an elaborate scheme to jail Holliday. With that done, he would then travel to Gunnison and maintain a close surveillance on Earp. Once the extradition papers were served, the net would close and the law would take its course. Earp and Holliday would rapidly, if reluctantly, he hustled aboard a train bound for Arizona.

On the stroke of ten, Starbuck entered the Slaughterhouse Saloon. Always punctual, Perry Mallan was waiting at a table in the rear. An ox of a man, Mallan was heavyset, with shoulders like a singletree. He looked tough as nails, and perfectly suited to the Slaughterhouse, the rawest busthead dive in all of Denver.

In truth, Mallan was a gentle soul, a frustrated actor, with a secret yearning to tread the boards. Lacking the stature to play Hamlet, he practiced instead the ancient art of chicanery. He was a swindler and confidence man nonpareil, and his performances had drawn rave reviews from every police department throughout the midwest. Starbuck had imported him from Chicago early last week.

Mallan was nursing a warm beer. Starbuck ordered one of the same, and waited until the bartender returned to his station behind the counter. Then he smiled, searching Mallan's face.

"All set for the big day?"

"You bet'cha," Mallan blustered. "It'll be a piece of cake."

"Got your papers?"

Mallan patted his coat pocket. He had a forged document, provided by Starbuck, which identified him as a Utah peace officer. He also had an outstanding murder warrant for one John H. "Doc" Holliday. There was a slight hitch in his voice when he spoke.

"You're sure the bulls won't tumble?"

"Dead sure," Starbuck affirmed. "Holliday's like a black-eye to Denver. The police will jump at the chance to put him behind bars."

Mallan looked worried. "I'm still not too keen on the next part. What if they release him to me? I'd play billy-hell taking him back to Utah."

"I've told you a dozen times. Holliday will hire himself a lawyer, and the whole thing's certain to get bogged down in the courts. You just stick to your story and tell everyone you've requested extradition papers."

"That's what bothers me. Somebody could get nosy and check with the Utah authorities. Then I'd be left holding the bag."

"No chance," Starbuck assured him. "It'll take weeks, maybe even a month, before anyone gets wise. By then, you'll be long gone and a helluva lot richer."

"I'll drink to that."

Mallan took a long draught from his beer stein. Starbuck leaned back in his chair, his legs stretched out before him. A moment passed while he studied the con man with an appraising look. For the past week they had rehearsed until Mallan had the story letter perfect. But now he seemed to have developed a case of the last minute jitters. At length, Starbuck leaned forward, elbows on the table.

"You got your pitch down pat?"

"Oh, sure," Mallan said hoarsely. "I could spiel it off backwards."

"Anything left to iron out? Now's the time to do it."

"No." Mallan sounded uncertain. "I'm as ready as I'll ever be."

"How ready is that?" Starbuck asked in a low voice. "You're not getting cold feet on me, are you?"

"Not on your tintype!" Mallan said indignantly. "I'm too old a hand for that. Nerves like a rock!"

"Cut the crap!" Starbuck said curtly. "Something's bothering you. Let's hear it, and don't give me any song and dance!"

"Well—" Mallan shrugged, his mouth downturned in a grimace. "All right, I'll be square with you, Luke. I'm a grifter, not a gunman! I've got the sweats about Holliday."

Starbuck waved the objection aside. "For Chrissake, you'll have the drop on him! What could go wrong?"

"Good question." Mallan gave him a hangdog look. "What if he decides to make a fight of it? I've never shot a gun in my life, much less a man. It's not my style!"

"Leave that to me," Starbuck said calmly. "I'll back your play straight down the line, and I don't miss. If he even looks cross-eyed, he's a dead man."

"I get the feeling you'd like that."

"Let's just say I wouldn't lose any sleep over it."

"Fair enough," Mallan said with a lame smile. "I'll be there on the dot of six. You just keep your eyes peeled in case he gets testy."

"Like you said," Starbuck noted dryly. "It's a piece of cake."

His beer untouched, Starbuck rose and walked toward the door. Mallan watched him a moment, wondering vaguely how the night would end. Then, with an unsteady hand, he quaffed the mug of beer in a single gulp.

Shortly before six, Perry Mallan stepped through the door of the Criterion. One of the Denver's plusher establishments, the Criterion was a high-class saloon and gambling casino. The front of the room was devoted to assorted games of chance, and several poker tables were ranged along the rear wall. Doc Holliday was seated at the center table.

Mallan exchanged a glance with Starbuck, who was standing idly at the end of the bar. Then he moved through the crowd and walked directly to the poker table. He halted on an angle that gave Starbuck a clear field of fire. Without hesitation, he pulled a bulldog pistol from inside his coat and leveled it on Holliday. The other players froze, their eyes glued on the gun.

"John H. Holliday!" Mallan said forcefully. "I have a warrant for your arrest."

"Arrest!" Holliday croaked, like a whorehouse parrot learning a new obscenity. "On what charge?"

"The murder of Charles Dunwood."

"Who?" Holliday glared at him in baffled fury. "I don't know anybody named Dunwood."

"You should," Mallan countered. "You murdered him in Provo, Utah, on August 8, 1878."

"Utah!" Holliday's eyes held a wicked glint. "I've never set foot in Utah! And who the hell are you, anyway?"

"Deputy Sheriff Mallan." Mallan cocked the bull-dog pistol. "I'd advise you to come along peaceable."

"Come along where?"

"To the police station, where formal charges will be lodged awaiting extradition to Utah."

"You're crazy." Holliday went white around the mouth. "I'm not going anywhere, especially Utah."

"Be warned!" Mallan boomed. "If you resist, I will be forced to shoot you dead where you sit."

Holliday hesitated, eyeing the snout of the pistol. Then, with an unintelligible oath, he drew himself up stiffly, hands raised. Mallan patted him down, tossing a Colt sixgun and a hideout stiletto on the table. All business, Mallan next spun him around like a top and shoved him hard.

"March! And no tricks if you value your life!"

Holliday marched. On the way past the bar, he gave Starbuck a look of muddled outrage. Starbuck lifted his hands in an elaborate shrug, and looked equally dumbfounded. Then the crowd parted and Mallan hustled his prisoner toward the door.

Outwardly sober, Starbuck gritted his teeth to keep from laughing. He thought to himself that Mallan had missed his calling. The man was a born stage actor, and a ham to boot. A regular goddamn Edwin Booth!

* * *

"When do you leave?"

"Tomorrow morning."

Horace Griffin pursed his lips and nodded solemnly. "Any chance Earp will run?"

Starbuck had gone directly from the Criterion to the Wells, Fargo office. He was seated now beside the superintendent's desk. He pondered the question a moment, then wormed around in his chair and flexed his shoulders.

"Always a chance," he conceded. "I'm counting on him to stay put once he hears it's a Utah warrant. Not very likely he'd connect that to the Arizona business."

"And if he does?"

"Then I'll stop him," Starbuck said evenly. "That's why I'm going to Gunnison."

Griffin gave the matter some thought. "There's still no indication," he said finally, "as to when we'll receive the extradition papers from Arizona. It could be tomorrow or it could be a month from now."

"I'll wait," Starbuck observed stoically. "Holliday's on ice, and Earp might as well be. Even if he spooks, he won't get very far."

"At this point," Griffin remarked, watching him closely, "the company would much prefer to see Earp stand trial. The publicity would serve as an excellent object lesson for stage robbers." He paused, weighing his words. "Don't kill him unless it's unavoidable."

"That's the only reason I ever killed anybody."

Starbuck rose and the superintendent gravely shook his hand. As he went out the door, Griffin frowned and settled back in his chair. A thought persisted, and he found himself unable to shake it off. He wondered how long Wyatt Earp had to live.

CHAPTER 19

The sun was a swollen ball of orange on the western horizon. The evening train from Denver chuffed into the Gunnison station and ground to a halt. The passengers, as usual, were a motley assortment drawn to Colorado's latest boomtown.

Starbuck was standing near the depot door. His wait in Gunnison had stretched to almost two weeks, and he was still operating undercover. Coded telegrams from Horace Griffin kept him advised of events at the state capital. Until yesterday, there had been little or no progress. Then a wire notified him that the extradition papers had been delivered to the governor in Denver. Another wire, arriving late this morning, instructed him to meet the evening train. The deciphered message gave him a description, and more importantly, a name. Sheriff Bob Paul of Tucson, Arizona.

Starbuck waited now under the overhang of the depot roof. The stationmaster was a nodding acquaintance, but he saw no one else who might recognize him. His eyes scanned the passengers debarking the train. Gunnison was growing rapidly, and every train was packed with new arrivals. The mix was generally split between workingmen and rogues. Tonight's lot was sprinkled with miners and drummers, but the sporting crowd, especially fancy ladies, was well represented. Like every boomtown, the lure was strongest for the most disreputable element. Vice was already the backbone of Gunnison's commerce.

One of the last passengers off the train brought Starbuck alert. The man stepped onto the platform and stood looking around. He was of medium height, solidly built, with angular features and a neatly trimmed mustache. He wore a broadcloth coat and a high-crowned Stetson, and he was carrying a battered warbag. Under his coat the bulge of a sixgun was plainly visible. He fitted the description in the telegram perfectly.

With a casual air, Starbuck moved from underneath the overhang and lit a cheroot. He glanced at the lawman over the flare of the match, and their eyes met. He ducked his chin, indicating Paul was to follow him. Then he turned and walked toward the end of the platform.

The main street of Gunnison was lined with saloons and stores and several greasy-spoon cafes. The evening crowds were already out in force, and the town hummed with activity. Halfway up the street was the Olympic House, one of three hotels already in operation. Starbuck sauntered along at an unhurried pace, weaving in and out of the throngs jamming the boardwalk. He felt certain Paul would keep him in sight, and he paused only when he reached the hotel. There, he glanced back and saw the lawman a few steps behind. A quick look was exchanged, then he entered the hotel.

Crossing the lobby, he mounted the stairs to the second floor. A central hallway ran the length of the hotel, and he moved rapidly to his room. He unlocked the door, stepping inside, and waited. The sound of footsteps grew louder, and a moment later Paul entered the room. Starbuck closed the door, locking it with a twist of the key. When he turned, the lawman was watching him with a fixed smile.

"No offense," Starbuck told him, "but I'd like to hear your name."

"Bob Paul," Paul said, hand outthrust. "If you're not Luke Starbuck, we're both in a lot of trouble."

Starbuck shook his hand warmly. "I'm damn glad to meet you. It's been a long wait."

"So I'm told." Paul tossed his hat and warbag on the bed. "Horace Griffin filled me in on the whole story. He says you've been doggin' Earp since last December."

"That's the way it worked out."

"Then you were with him the night he killed Frank Stilwell."

"It was more like an execution. Earp never gave him a chance, just cut loose with that shotgun."

"He's bound to hang, then! With you on the witness stand, we'll have an airtight case."

Starbuck waved him to a chair. "What's the latest on the extradition?"

"Looks good," Paul said, seating himself. "I left the papers with the governor's office yesterday. Griffin said he'd wire us the minute they're signed."

"Why didn't you wait and bring 'em along?"

"Politicians aren't much at keepin' secrets. Figured I'd come on here, just in case word leaked out to Earp."

"Sounds reasonable." Starbuck straddled a chair. "Speaking of politicians, how'd you leave things in Arizona? We heard you and Behan locked horns over who had first dibs on Earp."

Paul chuckled softly. "I finally convinced the territorial governor that I had the best case. Behan damn near tore Tombstone apart when he got the word."

"Wouldn't be surprised," Starbuck noted. "Earp made a fool out of him more times than you could count."

"Tell me about Earp," Paul said with a quizzical frown. "What's his game here in Gunnison?"

Starbuck gave him a slow, dark smile. "Leopards don't change their spots. He's got himself a faro concession at the Tivoli Saloon, and from what I gather, he's buying property hand over fist. Give him a little time, and he'll end up the town's leading citizen."

"How about politics?"

"Same as Tombstone." Starbuck shook his head ruefully. "Course, you've got to give him credit. He sizes things up and then he moves fast. No flies on him!"

"And folks buy it?" Paul said, troubled. "Don't they know all the stuff he pulled in Arizona?"

"Earp's a smooth article," Starbuck replied. "He gets close to the right people, and keeps telling them he was framed by Behan because he tried to run the criminal element out of Tombstone. Pretty soon they start believing it."

"What do you mean—the right people?"

"Well, for one thing, he's already in thick with a couple of the big mine owners. That's what I mean about a leopard. He's working the same dodge, damn near step-for-step, that he used in Tombstone."

"I hope to Christ—"

There was a knock at the door. Hitching back his chair, Starbuck motioned the lawman to the far side of the room. Then he walked to the door and opened it. A bellman handed him a telegram and accepted a dollar tip in return. Closing the door, he tore open the envelope.

"It's from Griffin."

While Paul watched, he took a pencil and slowly decoded the message. His expression turned grim, then gradually dissolved into a look of thunderstruck rage. At last, cold fury written across his features, he glanced up at the lawman.

"The governor refused to sign the extradition papers."

"On what grounds?"

"Legal technicalities." Starbuck studied the telegram a moment. "Griffin doesn't spell that out, but he says there was pressure brought to bear on the governor. Pressure not to extradite."

"Pressure!" Paul repeated. "Pressure from where?"

"Gunnison," Starbuck said in disgust. "Earp's evidently in thicker than I thought with the mine owners."

"But it's a murder charge!" Paul's eyes were rimmed with dull despair. "The evidence was all laid out, depositions and everything. How the hell could he refuse to extradite?"

"Who knows," Starbuck said woodenly. "Where politics are concerned, it don't pay to underestimate Earp. I should've learned that in Tombstone."

The truth suddenly came home to him. There was no way to touch Earp. Working within the law was a waste of time. With bleak irony, he asked himself why he'd even tried. Some men, using politics to insulate themselves, were above the law. Even in Arizona, had Earp been brought to trial, it very likely would have resulted in acquittal. There were too many skeletons that couldn't bear the light of day. Too many men of wealth and power who, as a last resort, would have called all their political markers in his defense. Only outside the law could Wyatt Earp be stopped. There was no legal way.

"How bad do you want Earp?"

"Pretty bad," Paul said slowly. "Why?"

"Because I'm fixing to handle this thing the way I should've handled it a long time ago."

"How's that?"

"Feet first." Starbuck's voice was edged. "You got any objections?"

"Objections!" Paul's laugh was a harsh sound in the cramped room. "Hell, I'll back your play!"

"It might cost you your badge."

"Would it get Earp killed?"

"If I can force him to draw," Starbuck said with surpassing calm, "he'll be dead before he gets the message."

"How d'you figure to do that?"

"He's got a weak spot. I aim to gig it till he sees red."

"When?"

"Tonight," Starbuck said, rising to his feet. "Let's go."

"Where to?"

"The Tivoli."

Upstreet from the hotel, the Tivoli Saloon was wedged between a dancehall and a two-bit a night flophouse.

By comparison with Denver gaming parlors, the Tivoli was crude and barnlike in appearance. Coal oil lamps hung bare from the rafters and the back bar mirror was webbed with cracks. The ubiquitous nude paintings were conspicuous by their absence, and the bar, though mahogany, looked as if it had been purchased at a bankruptcy auction. Spittoons were much in evidence, and sawdust covered the floor to absorb blood from the nightly slugfests.

While miners were not partial to guns, they took queer delight in maiming one another in no-holds-barred rough and tumble brawls. A bullet-headed bouncer, wearing an eye-patch and an evil grin, refereed the bouts with a lead-loaded bungstarter. He allowed the fights to go no more than a couple of rounds before he waded in and began splitting skulls. An ivory tickler, generally souped on rotgut whiskey, accompanied the thunk of his bungstarter on a rinky-dink piano. Such as it was, the bouncer and his musical colleague were the only entertainment in the Tivoli. The gaming tables, thought to be rigged, were considered more challenge than amusement. The miners spent their evenings trying to outguess quick-fingered dealers.

The bouncer was dragging a limp gladiator through the door as Starbuck and Paul entered the saloon. A raucous crowd already jammed the room, and the gaming tables were under siege by miners as yet unconvinced that the hand was quicker than the eye. Starbuck led the way to the bar, and bulled a spot for himself and the lawman amongst the serious drinkers. He chose a position directly across from Earp's faro layout.

Sipping whiskey, Starbuck turned his back to the bar, one heel hooked over the brass rail. Several minutes passed before Earp happened to glance in his direction. A ferocious grin lit his face and he rolled his eyes toward Bob Paul.

Earp followed his gaze and abruptly stopped dealing. From past meetings, he knew the Arizona lawman on sight. Once, during his brief tenure as a U.S. Deputy Marshal, they had even worked together in an effort to trap the Brocius gang. The faro game forgotten, his eyes hooded and his look suddenly became veiled.

"Wyatt Earp!"

Starbuck shouted the name. His abrasive tone claimed the crowd's attention like a clap of thunder. All eyes turned toward him and the buzz of conversation faded to watchful stillness. The men ganged around the faro layout slowly edged away. He pointed a finger directly at Earp.

"You're wanted for murder!"

Earp's expression was sphinxlike. He stared at Starbuck with eyes slitted against the smoky haze separating them. His voice was clipped, without inflection.

"What's your game, Johnson?"

"No game," Starbuck said, jerking a thumb at the lawman. "You know my friend here?"

"I know him."

"Course you do." Starbuck looked around at the crowd, grinning. "All the same, he ought to have a proper introduction. Gents, I'd like you to meet Sheriff Bob Paul, Pima County, Arizona. He's got a murder warrant for Earp's arrest."

"That's old news," Earp said tightly. "Everybody knows I was railroaded out of Arizona."

"So you say!" Starbuck's face took on a sudden hard cast. "What they don't know is that you're a garden-variety murderer. Common as dirt!"

"That's a goddamn lie!"

"No, it's the truth. You're no gunman, Earp! You've got everyone believing it, but that's the lie. You don't have the guts to meet a man face to face!"

"Watch your mouth, Johnson."

"Why? You aim to do something about it?"

Warren Earp, who was working the roulette wheel, stepped clear of the table. Countering his move, Bob Paul eased away from the bar, fixing him with a warning look. Silence thickened in the room. Open hostility was stamped on the Earp brothers' features, and a gunfight seemed inevitable. Then, at length, Earp shook his head.

"Something stinks here," he said gruffly. "Johnson, how come you're sidin' with a lawdog?"

Starbuck shoved off the bar. He crossed the room,

halting directly before the faro layout. There was a catlike eagerness in his eyes.

"I am a lawdog," he said with a cynical smile. "I work for Wells, Fargo."

Earp's composure slipped. His face became a mask of black and angry bafflement. "You no-good sonovabitch. You suckered me!"

"It was easy as pie," Starbuck taunted. "You're a tinhorn chiseler! Strictly smalltime."

No response.

Starbuck goaded him viciously. "Your whole family's smalltime. Your brothers are whoremongers! Your own wife's a whore. You're nothing but a bunch of penny-ante pimps! All of you!"

Earp's face was arrested in brute outrage. So complete was his shock that he appeared dazed, punchy. Yet he saw something in Starbuck's eyes that cut through his numbed senses. He knew his life was forfeit if he moved. The man standing before him was prodding him to draw, and be killed. He kept his hands plainly visible on the table.

Starbuck backhanded him across the mouth. His lip split, spurting blood, and a dread humiliation swept over him. But still he refused the challenge.

"Christ!" Starbuck said coarsely. "You've lost your balls, haven't you? You want to live so bad you'd take anything."

Earp merely stared at him, saying nothing. A moment passed, the crowd frozen in a spellbound tableau, watching them. Then Starbuck wagged his head back and forth.

"All right," he grunted. "Here's the way we'll play

it. You be on the morning train out of town. Otherwise
I'll kill you and take my chances with a jury."

Wheeling around, Starbuck pushed through the
crowd and walked toward the door. Bob Paul backed
along the bar, his eyes guarded, then turned and hurried outside. The miners looked stunned, like spectators at a public witch burning. They slowly moved
away from the faro layout, and Wyatt Earp.

The Tivoli closed early that night.

The sky lightened into cloudless dawn. The train stood
puffing steam and smoke before the platform. An eerie
quiet hung over the depot, and the passengers boarding
the train seemed strangely subdued. Once in their
seats, they crowded the windows, gawking at the two
men near the stationhouse door.

Starbuck took out the makings and built himself a
smoke. He lit the cigarette, inhaling deeply, savoring
the taste. Last night he'd thrown away the cheroots
and gone back to roll-your-owns. The act was a token
gesture, but nonetheless symbolic. He had laid Jack
Johnson to rest. Today, like slipping into an old shoe,
he was himself again. He thought it a damned comfortable feeling.

Bob Paul, standing beside him, stiffened as the stationhouse door opened. Earp, trailed closely by Warren, emerged and started across the platform. Starbuck
quickly moved forward and blocked their path. Without a word, he took the train ticket from Earp's hand.
Unfolding it, he studied the schedule a moment, then
looked up.

"California," he said, not asking a question. "I hear

there's ships there that go all the way to China."

Earp's expression was dour. "I reckon California's far enough."

"Think so?" Starbuck blew smoke in his face. "You just keep looking over your shoulder, Wyatt. One of these days you'll see me."

"What's your name?" Earp spoke through clenched teeth. "Who the hell are you, anyway?"

Starbuck grinned. "Death don't have a name. Now run along and catch your train before I change my mind."

Earp stepped around him and led Warren aboard the nearest passenger coach. The conductor signaled the engineer, and the locomotive chuffed a great cloud of steam. Wheels groaned and couplings cracked, and the train slowly got underway. As the caboose rolled past, Paul walked forward, halting at Starbuck's elbow. They watched, preoccupied with their own thoughts, until the train disappeared down the tracks. Then the lawman let out a heavy sigh.

"Too bad," he said glumly. "About Earp, I mean."

"Oh?" Starbuck's eyes were fixed upon distance. "What about him?"

"That he got away, beat the hangman."

"Maybe he only thinks he got away."

"What d'you mean by that?"

A cryptic smile touched one side of Starbuck's mouth. "Let's just say it's not over yet."

CHAPTER 20

Eagle City lay in the shadow of the Bitterroot Mountains. The town, not yet one year old, was the heart and hub of the Coeur d'Alene goldfields. The discovery had set off a mad stampede, and the small Idaho community quickly became the latest in a long string of western mining camps. Gold, the eternal magnet, drew adventurers by the thousands.

On a brisk autumn afternoon, Starbuck rode into Eagle City. His reputation as a detective was now legend throughout the West. Only last year, in perhaps his most celebrated case, he had broken a ring of train robbers in northern California. The reverberations shook the very power structure of San Francisco, involving political kingpins and warring Chinese tongs. The attendant publicity, with Starbuck's photograph splashed across dozens of newspapers, had robbed him forever of his anonymity. His face was known wherever he traveled, and he no longer undertook an assignment as himself. He was instead a master of disguise. A man of a thousand faces, none of them his own.

Today, like a chameleon, he blended perfectly with his surroundings. His appearance was that of a scruffy miner, a common day laborer. He wore a threadbare mackinaw, soiled trousers stuffed into mule-eared boots, and a woolen duckbill cap. His features were concealed beneath a wild shrub of a beard, and his hair sprouted down over his ears. He smelled rank as a billygoat and his jaw was ballooned by a wad of Red Devil chewing tobacco. His own mother would have disclaimed him.

His mission in Eagle City lacked official sanction. His disguise was not meant for payroll robbers or holdup men who plundered bullion shipments. Nor was he drawn by the lure of gold itself. He was there on personal business.

Starbuck was not a vengeful man. Yet he was proud, and by his own measure, he considered himself a man of character and worth. His reputation as a detective was the single most compelling force in his life. Once he accepted an assignment, he went about it with bulldog tenacity and an obsessive drive to emerge the victor. Failure was a word foreign to his lexicon, and defeat was anathema to his temperament. A deep and overwhelming sense of integrity dictated that once a job was undertaken he would see it through. He imposed no time limit on himself, and short of a complete reckoning, the case was never closed. However long it took, he earned his pay.

For eight years, he had served western business interests as a detective and professional manhunter. In all that time, despite the magnitude of the assignment, he had failed only once to deliver as promised. It was

a singular loss of prestige, and the one black mark on
an otherwise unblemished record. Today, he meant to
wipe the slate clean.

An item in the *Denver Post* had alerted him to old
and unfinished business. Not particularly newsworthy
in itself, the story carried a dateline of Eagle City,
Idaho. What made it of interest to Denver readers was
that it involved a man who, albeit briefly, was once
one of Colorado's more notorious citizens. The story
related that Wyatt Earp and three associates had recently been convicted of claim jumping in the Coeur
d'Alene goldfields. Tongue in cheek, the story went
on to state that Earp, at one time considered the terror
of Arizona, had now been reduced to petty misde-
meanors. The concluding paragraph posed something
of a question. Wondering aloud in print, it asked where
Earp had been keeping himself since his short, and
abruptly terminated, stopover in Gunnison.

Starbuck, in idle moments, had often pondered that
very question. Upon departing Gunnison, some two
years ago, Earp had simply dropped out of sight. Except for a fleeting sojourn to Dodge City, duly reported
by the Kansas papers, he had studiously avoided the
limelight. The reason was no great mystery to Starbuck. That last morning in Gunnison, at the train depot, he had warned Earp that the matter was by no
means settled. Earp, first and foremost a survivor, had
taken the threat seriously. Vanishing into nowhere, his
name had been all but forgotten by press and public
alike.

Yet now, the subject of an obscure news item, Earp
had surfaced once more. And Starbuck, unlike the

public, hadn't forgotten. The case was still open, and
the duebill was collectable on demand. In strictest confidence, he fired off a query to an old and trusted colleague in Idaho.

The reply, based on a week's investigation, was
much as he'd expected. Earp had arrived in Eagle City
shortly after New Year's. The gold camp was remote
and lawless, and he was soon up to his old tricks.
Forming a combine, he and three other men had begun
a campaign of outright intimidation. Some claim hold-
ers were persuaded to sell; those who refused found
their claims jumped and the property thereafter held
at gunpoint. Even when suit was brought, and the
combine was fined for claim jumping, the net effect
was unaltered. Earp, who apparently had no interest in
working the claims, sold out his interest. With a substantial stake, he then bought the White Elephant Saloon & Gaming Parlor. Ever the grifter, it was the kind
of goldmine Earp understood best. He relieved the
suckers of their poke over the gaming tables, and according to the report, he was doing very well indeed.
All in a matter of months, he had gone from claim
jumper to proprietor of the largest gambling dive in
Eagle City.

On the train ride north from Denver, Starbuck
found himself reflecting on the vagaries of time. Some
men's lives were touched by it, others were not. Doc
Holliday was now in a tubercular sanitarium, wasted
by disease and dying a lingering death. Warren Earp,
perhaps the best of all the brothers, had been killed in
a saloon shootout. But the head of the Earp clan, by
all accounts, had been affected little by the passage of

time. In some ways, Starbuck thought to himself, Wyatt Earp was like a pestilence. He infected those
around him, then moved on. He flourished while they
died.

Only Alice had escaped. Upon returning from Gunnison the summer of '82, Starbuck had set her up in
a millinery and dress shop. She proved a level-headed
businesswoman, repaying the loan with interest, and
they had kept company for nearly a year. When it
finally became apparent he would never settle down,
she proved equally realistic about her personal life.
After the long assignment in California, he returned to
Denver and found her engaged to a prominent attor-
ney. He wished her well, aware that she needed the
security of home and family, and even attended the
wedding. On occasion, when he was in Denver, he still
dropped by for a visit. She was radiantly happy, heavy
now with child, and time had done nothing to dim
their closeness. The memory of her often came to him
in strange places, when he was alone and without
friends. He cherished it in the way of a lonely man
compelled to travel a solitary road. Not with regret,
but with the warm remembrance of things past.

A week ago, before departing Denver, he had called
on her one last time. He told her nothing of his plan
to kill Earp. Any number of things might go wrong,
and he saw no reason to worry her needlessly. He had
every confidence he could outdraw Earp, but there was
always the chance he would himself die in the effort.
Bracing a man in his own saloon, where he was sur-
rounded by henchmen, entailed a high degree of risk.
Moreover, if his own identity was somehow discov-

ered, there was a good chance he would be charged with premeditated murder. For with some care, he had indeed calculated the death of Wyatt Earp.

Three days on the train, rattling northward, had done nothing to alter his resolve. Some men deserved to die, and Earp, more deserving than most, had been living on borrowed time. He thought it reasonable that he had appointed himself the instrument of Earp's death. By all rights, he should have ended it long before now.

Spokane, situated on the Washington-Idaho border, was the nearest train terminal to the Coeur d'Alene goldfields. There, at a livery stable, he had hired a horse and ridden toward the Bitterroots. His disguise was complete, and the plan, thoroughly rehearsed in his mind, was worked out to the last detail. Camped that night beside the trail, he slept the sound sleep of a man at peace with himself. He was ready.

Today, as he rode into Eagle City, his thoughts went no farther ahead than the next hour. He steeled himself to end it swiftly, without revealing either his identity or his purpose. The White Elephant, a clapboard building liberally doused with whitewash, was located in the center of town. He dismounted a couple of stores downstreet, and looped the reins around a hitch rack. Dusting himself off, he checked the Colt sixgun, snug against his belly in a crossdraw holster. Then he walked toward the White Elephant.

The layout in the gaming parlor was little different than he'd expected. A long bar fronted one wall. Keno, Chuck-a-luck, faro and roulette were ranked along the opposite wall. Poker tables, with baize-covered tops, were grouped at the rear of the room. The bar was crowded and the games were doing a brisk business. Several miners, dressed in rough garb similar to his own, were collected around the faro layout. He thought it entirely in character that Earp was dealing. He'd planned on it, and he hadn't been wrong.

Without pause, he moved straight to the faro table. He brusquely elbowed a place between two players standing directly across from Earp. Jostled aside, the miners cursed, on the verge of protesting. His pugnacious scowl seemed to invite trouble, and the men quickly decided to let it drop. He pulled a handful of gold coins from his pocket and looked over at Earp. His appearance was that of a grubby miner, and by pushing in at the table, he gave the impression of a short-tempered bully with an even shorter fuse. He saw no sign of recognition in Earp's eyes. To complete the ruse, he changed the timbre and inflection of his voice.

"This here game got a limit?"

"Fifty dollars," Earp replied calmly. "Bet 'em any way you choose."

"Aim to," Starbuck growled. "Gonna bust your bank, mister! Today's my day to howl!"

"Get a hunch, bet a bunch."

Earp indicated the table was open to play. Starbuck leaned across the layout and placed fifty dollars on the ace. When the other players had their bets down Earp dealt two cards, queen and deuce. He called the turn in a sing-song chant.

"The queen lays and the two spot pays."

"C'mon, deal!" Starbuck grunted testily. "Gimme an ace!"

Earp flashed him a look, but said nothing. The play continued, and Starbuck's luck, as though ordained, dovetailed perfectly with his plan. Always betting the ace, he lost one hundred fifty dollars within the space of eight turns. He fumed and cursed, one eye cocked askew each time an ace came up loser. On the eighth turn, watching his money disappear across the table, he fixed Earp with a sullen glare.

"You ain't listenin', dealer," he said hotly. "Ace to win, that's my play! Not the other way around."

"The cards talk," Earp said with a trace of irritation. "Place your bets, gents."

Starbuck slammed the last of his coins down on the ace. "Lemme see it! Gotta show this time!"

Earp dealt the cards. The case ace, the last in the deck, appeared first, a loser. Before the second card could be turned, Starbuck bristled and crashed his fist onto the table, scattering bets.

"Gawddamnit!" he roared. "I caught you!"

Earp's gaze narrowed. "Caught me what?"

"Caught you red-handed, you buttermouthed piss-ant! You're dealin' from a rigged box!"

"I run an honest game. I'd advise you to button up and back off."

"Honest, my ass!" Starbuck exploded. "You're slick, but you ain't that slick. I saw you kick out that ace!"

Earp appraised him at a glance. He saw no threat, merely a hotheaded trouble-maker spoiling for a fight. On sudden impulse, he decided to push it to the limit.

A sore loser, killed in a fair gunfight, would serve as a warning. A reminder that the White Elephant's square-deal policy was never to be questioned.

"One last chance," Earp said coldly. "Walk away or get carried away."

"You'd like that wouldn't you? Lemme go for my gun and your boys would backshoot me 'fore I even got started."

"We'll keep it private." Earp signaled the housemen to stay clear, then nodded to Starbuck. "All right, squarehead, just you and me."

"Wooeee! Let'er rip!"

Starbuck's hand snaked inside his mackinaw. The miner next to him, at that very instant, ducked and jarred his arm. He saw Earp's gun clearing the leather and he snapped off a hurried shot. Even as he pulled the trigger, he knew he'd missed the mark.

A splotch of blood blossomed on Earp's right coat sleeve, and his Colt clattered to the floor. He slammed backwards into the wall, arm hanging limp, his eyes bulging with shock. He stared across the table with a look of ashen terror.

There was a split-second when Earp's life hung in the balance. Starbuck wanted to kill him, felt some deep visceral need to kill him. But rational thought, not conscience, stayed his finger on the trigger. To kill a wounded man, standing helpless and disarmed, would make him fair game for the mob. Mining camps were infamous for their kangaroo courts and vigilante justice. Kill Earp and he would swing from a tree within the hour. There was no appeal, no court of last resort, in Eagle City.

Starbuck slowly lowered the hammer of his sixgun. He holstered it in a practiced motion, showing empty hands to the housemen. Then he leaned across the table, looking Earp straight in the eye.

"You don't remember me, do you?"

"I—" Earp shook his head, clutched painfully at his arm. "I don't know you."

"Yeah, you do," Starbuck said in his normal voice. "Think back, and it'll come to you. Gunnison, a couple of years ago, the train station."

"Johnson!" Earp croaked, his face a living wax-work. "Jack Johnson."

Starbuck gave him a strange crooked grin. One side of his mouth curled upward while the other remained set in a grim line. His eyes were cold as stone.

"Keep looking over your shoulder. We'll meet again."

Earp fainted. His eyes rolled back in his head and he toppled to the floor like a felled tree. Starbuck uttered a harsh bark of laughter. The housemen stared at him as though he were crazy, and the miners nearest the table seemed to shrink back in dread fear. A moment passed, then he turned and waded through the crowd. No one spoke and no one made a move to stop him. Halfway through the door, he suddenly wheeled around and fixed the room with a wintry smile.

"When he wakes up, tell him to sell out and take off running. I won't be far behind."

His laugh still lingered when the door swung closed. Later, men would say it was the laughter of death itself. The thought gained credence when Wyatt Earp sold the White Elephant to the first bidder. On

September 26, only ten days after being shot, he fled
Eagle City. His time in the western mining camps
ended there.

Outside town, Starbuck gigged his horse into a lope.
His smile vanished like a shutter being closed. He'd
put on a bold front in the White Elephant, but he felt
no elation now. He was wrestling instead with one of
life's great imponderables. A question that had dogged
him since his earliest days as a manhunter.

Today's shootout was no feather in his cap. No one
would record that his arm had been jostled, spoiling
his aim, and thereby sparing Earp's life. On the con-
trary, the incident would be twisted out of proportion,
facts interlaced with fiction, until it became scarcely
more than a pretzel of reality. Were Earp to live long
enough, the line separating truth from myth would
slowly diminish, ultimately disappear. That he had
been outdrawn and wounded, very nearly killed,
would be lost in the shuffle. He would emerge cloaked
in an aura of invincibility. A gunfighter who in the
end had proved unkillable.

Starbuck knew, from bitter experience, that truth
counted for little. His years as a manhunter had taught
him that people much preferred a candy-coated fairy
tale to the wormwood of cold facts. The public exhib-
ited some bizarre need for legends larger than life,
readily accepting the invention of dime novels as the
stuff of truth. Outlaws such as Jesse James and the
Youngers, portrayed as victims of injustice, were
transformed into folk heroes. Three years ago, when
he'd witnessed the death of Billy the Kid, he had seen

the process snowball with incredible speed. Virtually overnight, a mad dog killer had been canonized with all the attributes of an avenging angel. Once again, folklore and truth had joined hands in a fantasy concocted as a sugar-tit for the public.

Where Earp was concerned, the process assumed an added dimension. Truly great villains, who practiced murder and corruption on a wholesale level, were often remembered with more affection than dime-a-dozen outlaws. A dab of hypocrisy mixed with a dab of self-delusion very neatly whitewashed reality. Evil fascinated people, and they were prone to attach cardboard virtues to a scoundrel who dared greatly. With time, the murders at the OK Corral, the brutal executions of Frank Stilwell and Florentino Cruz, would be immortalized by penny-a-word hacks grinding out yet another potboiler. Wyatt Earp would emerge from the printed page a man of determination and grit, everready to enter where angels feared to tread. A frontiersman and gunfighter with all the mythical qualities of the breed.

Yet sainthood was rarely conferred on the living. There were exceptions, but more often than not a man was dead and buried long before the legend took form. Always the pragmatist, Starbuck thought the tradeoff was distasteful but nonetheless acceptable. He lived in the present, and events of some distant time were wholly beyond his control. For now, it was enough that Wyatt Earp died. He reaffirmed his vow that it would happen, and soon. He even took ironic amusement from the fact that he would hasten the legend.

In his own way, he would earn a niche in the dime novels.

The man who killed Wyatt Earp.

Westward lay the sunset of another day. He rode there, whistling softly to himself. All the yesterdays were behind him, and his thoughts turned toward tomorrow. Time meant nothing to the hunter, for time alone was his unalterable edge over the hunted. He idly wondered where they would next meet.

EPILOGUE

Starbuck and Wyatt Earp never again crossed paths.

Upon departing the Coeur d'Alene goldfields, Earp kept on the move. For the next thirteen years, seemingly always on the run, he roamed the West like a nomadic vagabond. He appeared briefly in Kansas, Texas, and Wyoming, never staying long in any one spot. Off and on, he returned to California, but only for short periods of time.

Then, in 1897, he joined the Alaska gold rush. He opened a saloon in Nome, and remained there for four years. Once more on the move, he spent the next half-decade wandering California and Nevada. Finally, in 1906, he settled in Los Angeles. He was fifty-eight years old, and living from hand to mouth. Police records indicate he was arrested at least once on a charge of vagrancy.

All these years Starbuck served in one capacity or another as a free-lance detective. Usually operating undercover, his assignments took him the length and breadth of the West. Yet chance, or what some men call fate, never brought him in contact with Earp. He kept an eye on the newspapers, and an ear to the grapevine, constantly seeking word as to Earp's whereabouts. His search was relentless, but in the end to no avail. Several times he narrowly missed his man, arriving in Tonopah or Goldfield, and twice in San Francisco, only days after Earp pulled still another vanishing act. At last, in 1911, he called off the manhunt.

True to form, Earp was arrested in July of that year on a bunco charge. A brief news item related that he and two confederates were charged with conspiracy to fleece a Los Angeles businessman out of $25,000. Starbuck, who was in California at the time, read the account with grim satisfaction. His search, after twenty-seven years, seemed finally to have ended.

Upon investigating, however, Starbuck lost his taste for the kill. Earp was now an old man, pushing sixty-four, and living a precarious existence. Under constant scrutiny by the police, he was out on bail on another charge when arrested for complicity in the bunco swindle. Starbuck felt nothing akin to compassion. Nor had he mellowed after all that time, even though Tombstone lay a quarter-century and more in the past. He simply couldn't bring himself to kill a toothless old grifter. The act seemed somehow beneath his personal sense of dignity, and he left Los Angeles before the conspiracy trial began. He would, in later years, deeply regret the decision to let it end there.

Wyatt Earp lived to be an octogenarian. He died at age eighty-one on January 3, 1929. To the last, he maintained that he had served law and order as a frontier marshal in Tombstone and the Kansas cow-towns.

By the late 1920s, hucksterism was part of the American scene, and there were many people willing to exploit the windy pipe-dreams of a doddering old man. Exactly as Starbuck had foreseen, the myth-makers ultimately convinced the public that Wyatt Earp was a noble lawman, a gunfighter of legendary proportions. Earp went to his grave with the sly satisfaction of a grifter who has played the big con, and won. The public swallowed the fairy tale whole, sinker and all.

Starbuck knew the truth. Yet he was a manhunter, with no great urge to justify himself or leave testament to his work. Thus he never committed his thoughts to paper and spoke no word of those long ago days in Tombstone. He tried instead to kill Wyatt Earp.

The day they laid Earp to rest he still carried the scar of Starbuck's bullet. He lived out his life thinking the name of the man who shot him was Jack Johnson.

Starbuck always thought it a damn fine joke.

**Before the legend,
there was the man . . .**

And a powerful destiny to fulfill.

On October 26, 1881, three outlaws lay dead in
a dusty vacant lot in Tombstone, Arizona.
Standing over them—Colts smoking—were
Wyatt Earp, his two brothers Morgan and
Virgil, and a gun-slinging gambler named
Doc Holliday. The shootout at the O.K. Corral
was over—but for Earp, the fight had just
begun . . .

WYATT EARP

MATT BRAUN

IN 1889, Bill Tilghman joined the historic land rush that transformed a raw frontier into Oklahoma Territory. A lawman by trade, he set aside his badge to make his fortune in the boom-towns. Yet Tilghman was called into service once more, on a bold, relentless journey that would make his name a legend for all time—in an epic confrontation with outlaw Bill Doolin.

OUTLAW KINGDOM

MATT BRAUN

**AVAILABLE WHEREVER BOOKS ARE SOLD
FROM ST. MARTIN'S PAPERBACKS**